Vernon Coleman's Dictionary of Old English Words and Phrases

An Essential Vocabulary of Traditional English for Language Lovers

Expand your vocabulary with exotic words which add zest and character to your writing and speaking. Vernon Coleman's Dictionary of Old English Words and Phrases is gloriously old fashioned and proudly politically incorrect; it is the unapologetic antidote to the dull, woke 21st century version of the English language and, as such, is not recommended for the hysterical, the woke and the over-sensitive.

By the same author

A list of around 100 books by Vernon Coleman (both fiction and non-fiction) can be found in the Bookshop on www.vernoncoleman.com

Dedication
As always, to my Wife, Love and Eternal
Sweetheart
My Beautiful and Brilliant Antoinette
Love of my Life

Note

I disclaim all responsibility for the fact that much of the language in this book may appear offensive and old fashioned and certainly very 'incorrect' by modern standards. This is because much of the language used in the 16th, 17th, 18th and 19th centuries was offensive and politically incorrect. Indeed, the concept of 'political correctness' had not been invented. People didn't worry so much about offending their friends, relatives, neighbours, acquaintances and strangers. Indeed, offending friends, relatives, neighbours, acquaintances and strangers seems to have been considered an essential part of life's fun. So, dear reader, absolutely no apologies from our ancestors and none from me either. Enter these pages and you enter the rough and tumble of another world.

Preface

When I started this dictionary I thought that it would not be a book to sit down and read unless you are the sort of person who enjoys reading dictionaries, thesauruses and books of quotations. I thought of it, rather, a book to keep by your bedside or chair-side to dip into at odd moments, during television advertisements or the dull bits of programmes which promised more than they delivered. But as the book proceeded my view of it changed, and by the time I was half way through, I had realised that the book was acquiring a personality of its own – rather different to the usual collection of words; it had become something of a social history.

I also realised that this book had become the sort of publication which has an added value as a source of entertainment, amusement and information; of the sort which I refer to as the 'I say, Hilda, listen to this' or 'You won't believe this, Gerald' variety. (Naturally, you can interchange the names if you don't know anyone called Hilda or Gerald). I spent 30 years of my life working as a columnist in what then was still referred to as Fleet Street (simply because that was where the major national newspapers all had their offices) and I received many letters from readers telling me how much they enjoyed reading out bits and pieces from my columns either to their (possibly long suffering relatives) or to chums in the pub (who were, I suppose, more likely to say 'enough'). And I also discovered that radio presenters used to read out pieces they found amusing and that many other newspaper columnists used to copy out bits which they thought their readers would enjoy. This was particularly likely to happen when I worked as the agony uncle on a tabloid Sunday newspaper. It occurs to me that it would be a delight if readers found themselves sharing titbits from this book with friends and relatives.

I started collecting Victorian and rarely used words when I began writing my series of books about the village of Bilbury in Devon. I have no idea why I did this since the books were (and are) set in the 1970s, but it seemed a fun way to spice up the language. As a result, I now have a large library containing around 100 old dictionaries, books of quotations, thesauruses and books of slang and curious old

English words. And, of course, printed matter, which is largely reliable, can always be supplemented with the internet, which is an endless and inspirational source of contradictions and confusions. Wherever possible I've tried to include a few etymological and historical references though I do have to admit that many etymological references probably owe as much to the imaginations of their originators as anything else.

This book is full of forgotten, out of use words, words which haven't (officially) been used since the 16th, 17th and 18th centuries, words which have been lost, abandoned, changed or suppressed and words which have changed their use since they were first introduced (the definitions I have given here are the original definitions). This is a book to take with you if you have an appointment where you know you will have to wait for longer than is decent or if you need to make a journey of indeterminate length. It is a book to dip in and out of; it is a book to entertain and to educate. You will, perhaps, be surprised at how many synonyms there are for 'girl', 'prostitute' and 'brothel' and how much time appears to have been spent in pubs and in teasing, tricking and performing complicated practical jokes – all of which doubtless took the place of social media. Skulduggery and stealing were commonplace and managed quite well without computers or the internet.

I hope this is a book which will, painlessly, help you expand your word power. These are words which are an essential part of the English language; a vital part of our culture and a part of our history which is endangered. Most of these words do not appear in standard, modern dictionaries and those that do are usually defined in other ways; as a result this book is intended as an essential supplement to a good, standard dictionary. Rogues, bawds, innkeepers, pimps, brothel keepers, whores, pickpockets and shoplifters had a surprisingly large vocabulary.

I have consulted every old, out of print dictionary I can find – there are far more of them than you might imagine. Dr Samuel Johnson was not the only person compiling a dictionary, and some of the volumes I've studied were published more than a century before Dr Johnson produced his famous opus.

I should add, en passant, that there is less agreement among dictionaries than you might expect; time and time again I have discovered that a word may mean one thing to one dictionary compiler and something quite different to another lexicographer. Similarly, it has to be admitted that spellings change – particularly for words which have been in use for a thousand years or so. When this happens, the only thing that can be said with certainty is that there is no correct spelling; there are only different spellings. You pays your money and you takes your choice. To make life easier for us both I have, generally, stuck to whichever spelling looks most logical and less of a trial. I should also point out (in what appears to now be a never ending litany of excuses, explanations and postscripts manque) that my dictionary is by no means complete and, probably never could be. The supply of forgotten, half-forgotten words seems unending, and probably is, and all words deserve to be remembered and enjoyed. If you find new words which you think I should have included please feel free to make a note of them in the margins of my text. It would be jolly if we could share new words on social media but I'm afraid we can't do this because I have been banned from all social media for the heinous and curious modern crime of telling the truth. (If you are curious you can find out more by reading my book 'Truth Teller: The Price'.)

I have also included one or two of the most popular street cries and details of some of the often cruel and invariably rather complicated practical jokes which were a major part of daily life in the centuries up until the year 1900. And I have included quite a good deal of slang, including a little Cockney rhyming slang (which I'm afraid I find quite boring), but I have omitted deeply offensive words since I assume most people won't want to use them and their presence would merely ensure that this, like many of my other books, gets banned or submerged in a hailstorm of one star reviews. I've had more than enough banning to last a lifetime, thank you very much, and it is my hope that this modest adventure into etymology will not worry the censors unduly. I hope that no reader will be offended by the inclusion of the slang in this book. I am not the first editor to be aware of the hazard such inclusions must inevitably pose. In 1793, When James Caulfield published his dictionary entitled 'Blackguardiana: or, a dictionary of rogues, bawds, pimps, whores, pickpockets, shoplifters' he ended his Preface with these words: 'The Editor likewise begs leave to add, that if he has the misfortune to run foul of the dignity of any body of men, profession, or trade, it is totally contrary to his intention; and he hopes the interpretations given to any particular terms that may seem to bear hard upon them, will not be considered as his sentiments, but as the sentiments of the persons by whom such terms were first invented, or those by whom they are used.' Caulfield, whose book was priced at 'one guinea in boards', said that he had collected words from numerous sources including 'The Bellman of London, first published in 1608, and other dictionaries of the 17th and 18th centuries.

Not that this book is just about etymology. It's also about social and cultural history. Read about the words and phrases on these pages and you will discover that within all sectors of society there was a healthy disrespect for authority. People often took the law into their hands if someone in their community broke the rules. This was as true for, say, soldiers or seamen as for gang members. They didn't run off to complain to a senior officer, or make an anonymous complaint on social media, but they merely operated their own form of rough justice.

Moreover, it is clear from these words that centuries ago citizens had different priorities: drinking, games, sex and community life were all vital parts of each individual's life. Social strata may have been more obvious but instead of hidden resentment there was a healthy upwardly directed disrespect. And it has to be admitted that the thieving was somehow more straightforward than the sort of thieving we say today. Pickpockets were rife, as were burglars, but the thieves operated on a physical rather than a mental level. Things have changed. Yesterday, for example, I received no less than 14 emails (from different sources) telling me that a parcel was waiting for me and that I needed to get in touch with the sender immediately. I also received an email telling me that my website would disappear from the ether unless I sent money to someone somewhere. And today my wife received an urgent phone call from a caller who told her that if she didn't take action (and ring a number she was given) within two hours then her mobile phone would stop working – permanently. The crooks get craftier and nastier with each day that passes.

My aim, and hope, (and I've been working on this book for many years so I'm entitled to a little hope) is that at least some of these words and phrases (most of which first saw the light of day in the 19th century or before) will be revived and will return to our currently rather dull communal lexicon, overladen as it is with abbreviations and modern, technical jargon which is too often pompous and incomprehensible while also being far less colourful. These words and phrases will, I hope, add fun to your language though I should, I suppose, warn you once again that the book might not be a perfect cup of tea for the easily offended and wearily politically correct.

Finally, do please remember that some of the words in this book have different meanings today. The meanings I've used in this book are the meanings that were in use a century or more ago.

Vernon Coleman

Bilbury, Devon

P.S Many of the words in this book are described as Old English or Middle English. Old English is generally described as the language of the Anglo-Saxons (up to the year 1150) while Middle English covers words which originated in the years between 1150 and 1470. Any word appearing after 1470 can, I suppose, be described as 'modern'.

P.P.S. Oh, and one other thing: if you know someone who is learning English please give them a copy of this book to help with their studies. You could, if you were so inclined, encourage them to learn these words and to use as many of them as possible in their daily work and play. I have to confess that I much look forward to hearing a pompous Frenchman (proud of his linguistic skills) using words from this book, and using them with that arrogant certainty and superiority that seems common among cunning linguists.

Abbess – madam in a brothel

Abbot – husband of an abbess

Abel wackets – blows on palm of hand with a twisted handkerchief; in a card game played according to 'abel wackets' rules, the winner is allowed to hit the loser as many times as he or she has lost games

Abrams – someone who pretends to be completely mad, quite insane, mentally disturbed, miserable or more than a trifle on the nervy side, so that they will be more successful when begging or in some other way claiming financial support from the State or a charity

Absquatulate – leave abruptly, usually in order to escape unwanted consequences (e.g. 'he absquatulated when her husband returned unexpectedly')

Academy – a billiard room (as used in Paris in 1885) or a brothel

Acarpous – sterile, barren (of fruit)

Accident – child born outside marriage

According to Cocker – affirming that something is correct (after the book 'Arithmetic' written by Cocker)

Acknowledge the corn – admit to a minor offence in order to give credence to a denial of a major offence. And so, for example, a man accused of stealing four horses and bags of corn might admit that he'd stolen the corn but deny stealing the horses. The principle here is a simple one: if accused of two crimes, admit to the lesser but deny the greater

Act of Parliament – small beer (an Act of Parliament, now sadly no longer with us, ruled that a landlord had to give every soldier five pints of small beer free of charge)

Acteon – cuckold (derived from the horns put on Acteon's head by Diana)

Adiposity – fat

Adscititious – supplementary, additional

Afters – puddings, sweets and pies. The usage originated in Devon where people were often so poor that there were no afters. In those circumstances the phrase 'bring in the afters' was said satirically rather than in hope

Against the grain – unwillingly

Agerasia – youthful appearance in an old person

All his buttons on – he is sharp and alert (usually said of an elderly person)

All a-cock – beaten or vanquished

All-a-mort – struck dumb

All my eye and Betty Martin – an expression of doubt; a suggestion that the speaker is exaggerating or lying. St Martin is the patron saint of beggars and the prayer to him begins: 'O, mihi, beate Martine'.

All my eye and my elbow – posh version of the Betty Martin saying above. Nudge nudge (with the elbow) and wink wink (with the eye).

Alley – a go between (from the French word 'aller', to go)

Ally Sloper – an elderly man worn out of by drink (who usually has a red nose)

Alphonse – a man who takes money from a woman older and richer than himself in return for what may politely be referred to as 'favours'

Altogether – nakedness (in the novel Trilby a young woman sits in the altogether)

Ambidexter – a lawyer who takes fees from both the defendant and the plaintiff and is, therefore, probably of little use to either

Amen corner – church

Amen curlers – preachers or parish clerks

Amuse – to fling dust or snuff in the eyes of someone you are going to rob (also to invent a plausible tale in order to con someone out of their goods or money)

Anachronism – something belonging to another period; first used in the early 19th century

Anaphelosis – morbid state due to extreme frustration

Anathema – someone or something much disliked ('he was an anathema to me')

Anatomy – a poorly nourished individual of any age

Anchorite – hermit

Andiron – one of a pair of metal stands designed to support wood burning in a fireplace

Angel – a woman of the town (taken from the abundance of such women who used to be found in the Angel district in London)

Angel-makers – baby farmers

Angels on horseback – fricasseed oysters, wrapped in bacon and served with toast

Angler – petty thief or pilferer

Ankle – a girl who is pregnant but who wishes to hide the fact while requiring an excuse for her absence from professional or social life may be said to have 'sprained her ankle'

Anti-tox – a medicament given to sober up a drunk

Any work for John Cooper – travelling coopers could be heard advertising for work (by shouting this slogan) for several centuries up until the end of the 19th century; wooden tubs and pails were in general use and often needed mending

Ape leaders – elderly spinsters

Apophthegm – maxim, aphorism, epigram; all of which are easier to pronounce or spell than apophthegm which, to be honest, sounds more like an unpleasant respiratory condition

Aporia – irresolvable conflict within a text or theory

Aposiopesis – suddenly stopping in the middle of a speech (invariably a device or piece of trickery by the speaker to ensure he has the attention of his audience)

Apothecary – apothecaries (the forerunners of GPs) were not highly respected and the word was used to describe anyone who made an effort to look and sound as if they knew what they were talking about while talking gibberish

Apotheosis – the climax of something (a career, an event, a festival)

Apples – Cockney rhyming slang for stairs (as from 'apples and pears')

Archer up – congratulations (taken from the success of a jockey of that name in 1881)

Arf-a-mo – half a moment

Arf-an-arf – mixture of porter and ale

Arkansas tooth pick – a Bowie knife

Armour – condom, 'to fight in armour' meant 'to make use of Mrs Philip's ware' (Mrs Philip was the top maker and seller of condoms in London in the 18th century)

Asseveration – serious statement made solemnly and with great emphasis

Ataraxia – serene calmness

Atavism – someone who reverts to ancient habits and behaviour

Attercop – spider

Aunt – madam or brothel keeper

Aunt Sally – a black faced doll

Aunt's sisters – ancestors

Autem mort – married

Away – if a man (or woman) is in prison it is polite to say that he (or she) is 'away' from home; knowing and understanding relatives or friends will know not to ask questions

Awkins – a serious, severe man (not one considered game for a laugh); the phrase is taken from Sir Frederick Hawkins who was regarded as a hanging judge and therefore not to be taken lightly

Axe to grind – wanting a favour (a man pretending that he wanted to grind his axe was really angling for a drink)

B

Babes in the wood – rogues sitting in the pillory or the stocks

Baby and Nurse – two penny-worth of gin in a small bottle of soda water

Back biter – someone who slanders another behind his back or in his absence

Back gammon player – a sodomite

Back-hairing – women who, when fighting, take hold of the hair at the back of each other's heads are said to be 'back hairing'

Back of the green – theatrical term for 'behind the scenes'

Back row hopper – someone who enters a public house, pretending to be looking for a friend but hoping to be offered a drink

Backs – the backs of Cambridge colleges seen from the other side of the river Cam

Backsheesh – a bribe or 'present'

Bad egg – thoroughly disreputable person (as opposed to a 'good egg')

Bad hat – a disreputable person, not to be relied upon

Badger – to worry someone (as in worrying a badger in his hole to draw him out, though why anyone would want to do this is rather a mystery)

Bag and Baggage – completely

Bagpipe – to bagpipe was described by James Caulfield in his dictionary as 'a lascivious practice too indecent for explanation', and so, if it was too indecent for Mr Caulfield then I fear that we must leave the bagpipe to your imagination

Bags o' Mystery – sausages (only the person making a sausage knows what it contains)

Baker's Dozen – thirteen (in the reign of Edward I, bakers were subject to strict laws and could be severely punished if they sold a dozen loaves but only provided eleven – to avoid this danger they gave thirteen loaves when selling a dozen.) This explanation alone is surely worth the price of this book. Mr Caulfield reckons that a baker's dozen was fourteen not thirteen

Balaclava – a full beard (as seen on soldiers returning from the Crimea, hence the name). It was fashionable at that time for men to shape their beards in some way, so full beards were unusual

Balderdashing – mixing drinks (many years ago it was customary to combine beer with milk, later it became common to mix beer and wine. A punch is balderdash.)

Ballum rancum – a hop or dance at a brothel, where all the women are prostitutes

Banbury – a tart, and hence a loose women

Banbury story of a cock and a bull – roundabout nonsensical story

Bangs – fixed curls fixed over the forehead, introduced by the then Princess of Wales in the later years of the nineteenth century

Baptised – rum, brandy or any other spirits that have been diluted with water (spirits treated this way were also said to have been christened)

Barbecue – any large animal, fish or bird cooked whole

Barbermonger – fop with a fancy, expensive haircut (the word was first used by Shakespeare in King Lear)

Bark – squeal; inform the authorities about someone

Bark up the wrong tree – to be mistaken; this is an American phrase derived from the habit of using dogs to drive a racoon up a tree and then concentrating your energies on the wrong tree

Barker – employee of a dealer in second hand clothes; the barker would walk in front of the shop and deafen passers-by with his cries of 'clothes, coats or gowns'

Barking irons – pistols

Barkis is Willin' – proposal of marriage – taken from 'David Copperfield' by Charles Dickens

Barm – the froth on fermenting malt liquor (that's beer)

Barmicide – someone who promises much but provides little; first appearing in the English language in the early 18th century, barmicide is derived from Barmaki, a prince who appears in the Arabian Nights Entertainment; Barmaki, who regarded himself as a practical joker, invited a starving beggar to a meal but then presented him with a series of extravagantly served courses, each consisting of ornate dishes – which were empty.

Barmy – just a bit mad, cracked or potty (taken from St Bartholomew – the patron saint of mad people)

Barn stormer – second rate actor who plays in barns rather than a properly equipped theatre

Baron Munchausen – the amazing hero of a book which was written (in English) by a German called Rudolph Erich Raspe. In Raspe's book, published in 1785, Munchausen tells extravagant tales of his travels and abilities. In real life there was a Baron Munchausen. He lived from 1720 to 1797 and served in the Russian Army. He too told extravagant tales of his travels and abilities. (There is now a psychiatric disorder known as 'Munchausen's Syndrome'. Patients with this syndrome feign serious illness in order to obtain hospital treatment and some have been so convincing that they have been through numerous serious surgical operations. When I was a junior hospital doctor, we had biographies of some well-known patients with this syndrome stored in the Accident and Emergency department, and although they changed their names and appearances, the individuals rarely changed the diseases from which they claimed to suffer. There is also a condition known as Munchausen's Syndrome by Proxy in which parents claim that their children are ill when they are not.)

Bash – to hit someone hard but with your fist only

Basket making – a euphemism for copulation

Basket of Oranges – pretty woman

Baste – beat

Bastile – a prison or workhouse

Bath Oliver – a biscuit (the recipe for which was invented by a Dr Oliver of Bath)

Bathukolpian – large or deep breasted (taken from the Greek and first appeared in the English language in 1825; it was described as 'rare' in the massive two volume first edition of the Shorter Oxford English Dictionary on Historical Principles

Battology – unnecessary repetition of the same words or phrases, either in speech or in writing

Batty-fang – to give someone a thorough thrashing

Bavardage – idle gossip, derived from the French word 'barvarder' (to chatter)

Bawbles – testicles

Bawcock – term of friendship used between men as in 'hello, my old bawcock'

Bawd – brothel keeper or female pimp

Bawdy-Basket – female crook; most bawdy baskets sold pins, tape, ballads and obscene books but lived mostly by stealing

Bawdy House Bottle – short measure sold to bawdy house customers who either didn't notice or didn't care that they were being cheated

Bayreuth Hush – complete silence, as might be expected at the Opera House in Bayreuth when a Wagner festival is about to start

Beanfeast – a treat; a ripping good time had by all (originally, a beanfeast was an annual treat provided by employers and consisting of broad beans and boiled bacon); eventually a beanfeast was reduced to a 'beano'

Bear – someone who sells stock (shares) that he doesn't own

Beard splitter – man 'much given to wenching'

Beast with two backs – another euphemism for copulation

Beau – a fashionable man, greatly concerned with his appearance

Beau trap – loose stone in a pavement under which water collects; when trodden on, water squirts up and damages the beau's white stockings

Bed – to put to bed with a mattock and tuck up with a spade is to bury someone (to go up a ladder to bed is to be hung)

Bee – a meeting where people (usually women) do things such as make quilts or pick apples

Been to see Captain Bates? – a question commonly asked of someone not seen for a while (Captain Bates was a well-known prison governor)

Beer and skittles – a synonym for having a darned good time without the broad beans and the bacon which characterised a beanfeast; later the words 'life isn't all…' were added and used to imply that life isn't always just good times (as if anyone needed reminding)

Beer–bottle – a stout man with a ruddy face

Beer-eater – someone who drinks a good deal of beer

Beer-jugger – a barmaid

Before the War – when times were better (it doesn't matter which War is referred to since any War will do and the phrase goes back a long way)

Beggar makers – ale house, or pub

Begorra – used as a solemn Irish oath

Belch – beer (since beer tends to cause eructation)

Bell the Cat – taking a risk to make progress (the saying comes from the fable which describes how mice decided to hang a bell around a cat's neck so that they would be warned when the cat approached – the problem was: who would 'bell the cat'?)

Bellibone – Dr Johnson, who knew a thing or two about words, described this one as meaning 'a woman excelling both in beauty and goodness'; despite the good doctor's enthusiasm the word seems to have disappeared

Bellicose – bad tempered, violent

Belly cheat – apron

Belly plea – plea of pregnancy offered by female felons to help them avoid the gallows (there were said to be warders in all gaols who would make female prisoners pregnant for this purpose)

Belly washer – lemonade or fizzy water

Bell wether – chief or leader of a mob (the phrase is taken from flocks of sheep – where the 'wether' has a bell around its neck)

Belt – to assault someone (in the English army belts were readily used as weapons)

Belvedere – turret, room with windows for looking out, a room or a place with a view

Ben – a lie (Ben is short for Benjamin Trovato – mentioned in an Italian proverb)

Bend o' the Filbert – a nod of the head (from the fact that the head is sometimes called the nut)

Bender – drunken spree

Bet you a million to a bit of dirt – a dead cert

Bet your boots – a safe bet (since boots were always valuable)

Bezzle – to drink and to behave in a sottish manner (note 'sottish' and not 'Scottish')

Bible class – a man with two black eyes was said to have been to a bible class

Bibliolatry – worship of books

Bibliotaph – someone who hoards books

Biddy – chicken, young wench

Bidet – described in the 18th century as 'a kind of tub, contrived for ladies to wash themselves for which purpose they bestride it like a little French pony or post horse'

Bifarious – facing both ways; someone who will support anything and who will change their mind whenever they see a chance to improve themselves by so doing

Big bird – hissing heard in a theatre if the audience was unhappy (a goose hisses and is a big bird)

Big end of a month – three weeks

Bilk – to cheat (as in 'I've been bilked by the grocer/whore/coachman')

Billy Goat in Stays – term of contempt

Billy Turniptop – agricultural labourer

Bin – mineral spring

Birmingham School – used to refer to radical views ('the Birmingham School of thought')

Biscuit and Beer Bet – a swindle common in pubs (the victim is given a dry biscuit to eat and the bet is that his opponent can drink a glass of beer with a teaspoon faster than the victim can eat the biscuit – the biscuit is so dry that the beer drinker invariably wins)

Bit o' Blink – drink (rhyming slang)

Bit o' Crumb – good looking plump girl

Bit o' Haw Haw – fop

Bit o' Jam – pretty girl

Bit o' Pooh – nonsensical flattery; blarney

Bit o' Raspberry – attractive girl

Bit o' Stuff – good looking woman

Bit o' Tripe – wife (from rhyming slang)

Bitch the pot – pour out the tea

Bite off more than you can chew – take too large a bite of chewing tobacco

Bits of Grey – elderly folk present at social events to give dignity to the proceedings

Bits of Soap – charming and friendly girls

Bivvy – beer (from the French 'buvez')

Black-ball – to reject an applicant for club membership (The electors had a white ball and a black ball and were invited to put one ball into a closed box. If, when opened, the box contained one or more black balls then the applicant was rejected but no one would know who was responsible.)

Blackleg – someone who doesn't go on strike when his colleagues do

Black-silk Barges – stout women who dress in black in the probably mistaken belief that it makes them look thinner if not actually svelte

Blarney – flattery (named for the stone sticking out of a ruined window at the ruined Blarney Castle – those who risk their lives to kiss the stone are said to have the everlasting gift of 'blarney' – this custom is now around four hundred years old and as daft now as it ever was.)

Bless me soul – a Puritanical plea, derived from the words 'Bless me Saul'

Blessing – a tip or gratuity

Blind excuse – a not very good excuse

Blister – to punish (as in 'I'll blister him when I catch him')

Blizzard Collar – a high stand up collar which suggests that the wearer fears that cold weather is coming

Bloater – fat man or woman (named after the fact that when herrings are smoked they swell up to become 'bloaters' or, more specifically, Yarmouth bloaters)

Block – either a policeman or the young shapely girl in the linen department of a big store who tries on clothes to show potential buyers what they look like when worn. The policemen are still with us but the shapely girls have gone on to other things and are now probably working as influencers on one of the social media channels

Block a quiet pub – to sit in a pub for a long time

Blockhead – stupid person

Blockish – stupid when referring to a person; bulky and ugly when referring to a building

Bloke – friendly chap; reliable fellow who is on the way to becoming a mate

Blood – riotous and disorderly fellows

Blood or Beer – challenge to a friendly fight for a drink ('Take off your coat' is an invitation to a pugilistic encounter)

Bloody back – jeering name for soldiers (referring to their scarlet coats)

Blood-worms – sausage in general but black pudding in particular

Bloomeration – illumination

Bloomers – loose ankle length trousers worn under a skirt and originally designed to preserve the modesty of women riding bicycles (named after Amelia J Bloomer, a 19th century feminist, but created by the now largely forgotten Mrs Elizabeth Miller)

Bloviate – say a great deal without saying anything, as illustrated by TV talk show hosts, members of the royal family and celebrities in general

Blower – mistress or whore

Blow-out – feast

Blow the groundsils – make love on the ground or floor

Blowsa-bella – a vulgar, assertive woman; usually a stout one

Blue – miserable

Blue blanket – the sky (as in 'we slept under the blue blanket')

Blue pidgeon fliers – thieves who steal the lead off houses and churches

Blue pig – whisky (when requested in America in a temperance state or conurbation)

Blunge – to make a mess of something

Boarding school – any prison or house of correction

Bob – shoplifter's assistant (the one who carries off the stolen goods)

Bob, Harry and Dick – hungover and feeling sick

Bobby – faithful, reliable person (the name comes from Greyfriars Bobby, the devoted terrier who stayed at his master's grave in Edinburgh for twelve years and who aroused such affection that a kindly Miss Burdett Coutts erected a monument to his memory)

Bobby – policeman; named after Sir Robert (Bobby) Peel who organised the police force in London; policemen were therefore also known as peelers

Bodacious – admirable or attractive

Bodice – the part of any item of clothing which is above the waist, but not including the sleeves

Bodice-ripper – historic, romantic and sexually explicit novel in which a bodice may well be ripped, usually with the permission of the wearer

Body lining – strong twill used to line a bodice (probably unsuitable for bodices which are due to be ripped)

Bog house – defined as 'the necessary house'

Bohemian bungery – pub patronised by unsuccessful authors, of whom there are many

Boiled Owl – drunk (as drunk as a boiled owl, though there is no evidence that owls, boiled or otherwise, are likely to be intemperate)

Boko – large nose (an individual with a generously proportioned proboscis may be referred to as Boko)

Bone – thin man

Bone clother – port wine, which has (or had) a probably unjustified reputation for building muscle

Bone orchard – cemetery

Bone shaker – very early bicycle, which gave a rather uncomfortable ride

Bono Johnny – a decent bloke

Bonse – head (popular among schoolboys)

Boobies – breasts (there is an almost infinite number of synonyms for breasts in Old English, Middle English and Victorian English)

Boobies' Hutch – a place in military barracks where soldiers can drink when their canteen in closed

Boobocracy – government by the uneducated and the ignorant; government by boobs; first used in the early 20th century

Booby – awkward lout, clodhopper or yokel

Boodle – money

Boo-ers – theatre critics sitting in the gallery who would boo because it was easier and louder than hissing (the old, traditional show of dissatisfaction). Competitors and enemies of a theatrical management would sometimes hire boo-ers to disrupt a performance. (The word 'boo' was named after Captain Bo, a soldier who terrified the enemy with his voice)

Boon – a gift or favour (see Crave a boon)

Boot – money (the word 'boot' was originally used in this way by tailors and boot-makers in the same way that grocers referred to money as 'sugar' and milkmen use the word 'cream')

Booze-shunter – beer drinker

Borborygmy – an audible rumbling in the bowels; usually blamed by the owner of the noisy bowels on the dog or someone sleeping nearby (those permanently afflicted with this condition often acquire a dog so that they have someone to blame for the noises they make – 'Oh that dog is a constant embarrassment!')

Bosh – adulterated food and the adulterants themselves; in speech 'bosh' means merely nonsense

Bosom bottle – in the 19th century women used to wear flowers in their cleavage; the flowers were usually held in place within a bosom bottle, a silver cone covered with ribbon, which was lodged between the breasts; the bosom bottle sometimes contained a little water to keep the flowers looking fresh

Bosomy – having breasts which dominate, usually through size but sometimes through presentation

Bottle ache – hangover

Bottled – trapped, imprisoned, kept in one place or arrested (derived from the way the American fleet bottled up the Spanish fleet in Santiago by closing the narrow opening to the harbour)

Bought – used as a term of disparagement, since it was always thought that home-made items were always better than anything made in a factory or sold in a shop. Country houses used to have many members of staff to spin, to weave, to knit stockings and to plait straw as well as to bake bread, grow vegetables and rear animals

Bouguereau quality – obviously and rather outrageously effeminate (often used to describe art of all kinds)

Bouilli – boiled meat

Boulevard-journalist – an unscrupulous writer, usually working for a small journal which published scurrilous material ('journaux des boulevards' first appeared in France)

Boulevardier – a man pretending to be a man about town, a gentleman, though in reality a rather third rate fellow (based on the man about town in Paris)

Bounce – brag or boast or tell an improbable story

Bounder – dishonourable person, usually male

Bow-wow-mutton – terrible meat that might well be from a dog

Bowdlerise – censor (the word came from Thomas Bowdler 1754-1825, a publisher who censored works by Shakespeare and others – removing the bits he deemed offensive)

Boy Jones – secret informant. The original Boy Jones was a chimney sweep who tumbled out of a chimney at Buckingham Palace and was suspected of having heard State secrets being discussed by Queen Victoria and Prince Albert. This incident dramatically accelerated the use of brushes and other equipment to clean chimneys, rather than sending up small boys to dislodge the soot

Box coat – large, warm overcoat worn by coachmen (who had to sit up high and out in the cold)

Box the compass – to be able to recite the points of the compass and to be able to answer questions based on the divisions of the compass

Boycott – refusal to do something; (named after Captain Boycott, an Irish land agent who charged what the locals thought was too much and so they cut off his food and supplies – 900 soldiers were required to rescue the victim of the first boycott)

Braciere – the French word for the arm protection on a military uniform – it is wrongly thought by some that this word may have developed into the word brassiere which was adopted by English speakers

Bracket face – ugly man

Bradshaw – someone very precise and good at figures; taken from Bradshaw's Railway Guide, without which no Victorian traveller would dare set foot out of doors

Braggart – someone who boasts a good deal

Brass – money (the commonest term for metal money)

Brass up – to pay

Brassiere or bra – There is some confusion about who invented the bra (even Mark Twain is reported to have played a significant role) and both the French and the Americans have star candidates for the creation of the modern bust supporter. The importance of the bra in our modern world is signified by the fact that the bra department in some branches of Marks and Spencer (a major chain of high street stores in the UK) is bigger than the entire men's wear department. The word 'brassiere', which was borrowed from the French, actually refers to a baby's vest

Braxy – meat from a sheep that has died of natural causes or had an accident

Bray (vicar of) – someone who changes his principles and always allies with the strongest party

Bread and butter – sex in the missionary position

Bread basket – stomach. You will not be surprised to hear that in Ireland the equivalent word for stomach was 'tater-sack'

Break a leg – a woman who had a bastard child was said to have broken a leg

Breakdown – a type of dance, done without moving far from one spot. The word was first used to describe the failure of a piece of machinery in 1883 when a newspaper reported 'the breakdown of an excursion train'

Breaking shins – borrowing money

Breast fleet – a Roman Catholic (the phrase comes from the believe that Roman Catholics were known to beat their breasts when confessing their sins)

Breastsummer – large beam, usually made of oak, over a large opening

Breath strong enough to carry coal – drunk

Breeches – whoever wears the breeches (man or woman) is in charge of a relationship

Bricky – brave, fearless person (male or female); in short, 'a brick'

Bridgeting – obtain money under false pretences from servant girls. The term is derived from the fact that in Ireland many girls were named after Saint Bridget. It duly became common for all domestic servants to be known as 'Bridget' (possibly because this made it easier for employers who didn't have to bother themselves remembering the names of their staff). Tricking servant girls to part with the very little money they had seems pretty low

Brief – piece of paper with writing on it; any letter or document and not just a document provided for a barrister

Brigandine – body armour, primitive form of corselet; made of metal rings sewn on canvas

Brim – fearless woman of the town (the phrase 'woman of the town' is not much of a compliment)

Broad-gauge Lady – a woman who is wide enough to make a railway seat rather crowded

Broken Brigade – 'stone-broke' younger sons living on their wits

Broom – someone pretending to be a 'swell'

Brother starling – a man who lies regularly or only with the same woman (i.e. makes a nest and sticks with it)

Brouhaha – noisy and overexcited critical response, lot of publicity

Brown study – thought and speculation

Brownies – cigarettes (usually costing three for a half penny; nothing to do with chocolate buns or small girls pitching tents and cooking sausages on open fires)

Bub – husband or a boy (popular in America where husbands are treated as boys though boys are not, generally speaking, treated as husbands)

Bubble – to bubble is to cheat and the word has been used thus since the days of Queen Anne

Bubble and squeak – beef and cabbage (so called because it bubbles and squeaks when cooked over a fire)

Buck against – to oppose (derived from the bucking nature of goats and stags)

Buck parties – social events for bachelors, regarded as rather uncivilised social events (the origins of 'stag parties' are clear)

Bucket – to kick the bucket is to die

Bucking the tiger – to gamble heavily

Buck's face – cuckold

Bud – young girl

Budge – also known as a 'sneaking budge', a budge is someone who slips into houses in the dark to steal cloaks or other clothes

Budge doctors – doctors' robes, usually made of lamb's fur

Buffy – drunk; as in 'he came home buffy every Saturday night'

Bulk and file – pair of pickpockets; the 'bulk' jostles the individual to be robbed and the 'file' does the stealing

Bull – someone who buys stock or shares on speculation, hoping that the price will go up

Bullion – gold or silver measured by weight (not to be confused with bouillion)

Bullycock – someone who starts a quarrel in order to rob the people who are quarrelling

Bullyrag – scolding that goes on and on and on; it is customary for a wife to bullyrag a husband, though in fairness it has to be said that in many cases he probably deserves it

Bullytrap – brave man who falsely appears mild or effeminate and who, thereby, takes in bullies who wrongly see him as easy prey

Bum brusher – school master

Bumblepuppy – an old-fashioned game which first gained popularity in 1801; the idea was to roll small balls into nine holes made in the ground, with each hole having a separate scoring value; the game was popular in public houses which sometimes had specially prepared holes with small round pebbles playing the part of the balls; the game of 'nine holes' has been traced back to 1534, though it might be older; today the noun bumblepuppy appears to be used for a game played with a ball attached to a post; the idea is for one or two players to keep the ball in motion

Bumblesome bumblebug – clumsy person

Bumbo – brand, water and sugar

Bumfluff – tedious and useless printed material; originated in the late 19th century from the slang 'bum-fodder'; originally related to advertising leaflets and pamphlets but can now be suitably applied to the printed material produced by the mainstream media, political parties and (especially) local councils

Bummer – commercial traveller, salesman, company representative

Bun feast – a rather miserable 'party' or feast, where buns are pretty much the only comestibles on display

Bunch of fives – fist

Buncombe or bunkum – flattery, nonsense; a politician's promise

Bundling – courting done while both parties are prone, though what they are prone to do is not for discussion here

Bung – a term of endearment or abuse, depending upon the originator and the target, and their relationship; a landlord might be called a bung, as might a publican

Bunk – verb, to retreat or escape

Bunko – doubtful, dodgy (a confidence trickster might be known as a bunko man)

Bunkum – insincere nonsense, balderdash, claptrap; the insincerity inherent in the definition suggests that 'bunkum' should be used to describe the claptrap emanating from the mouths of politicians

Bunter – a female thief, a prostitute or a beggar; also a pregnant girl (perhaps from the idea that some female thieves might stuff stolen goods down their skirt or dress in the hope that the lump will be mistaken for signs of a pregnancy)

Burning shame – lighted candle stuck into the private parts of a woman (though for what possibly reason I cannot begin to imagine – other than the absence of another more usual candle holder)

Burnt – an individual with the pox or the clap (word commonly used by seamen)

Burst – crowd of theatre-goers leaving a theatre after the final curtain

Burst her stay-lace – an indignant woman might do this, as might a tightly laced woman struggling for breath; it was not unknown for a woman literally to break the laces of her corset (possibly to her relief)

Bury – to desert; 'he buried his wife' means he deserted her

Buryen face – solemn look (a burying face)

Bus – badly made, dowdy dress suitable only for someone who travels on public transport

Bushel bubby – full breasted woman

Busnacking – interfering (as in 'I wish Mrs Jenkins would stop busnacking')

Buss me – kiss me (from the French 'baise moi')

Bust – large drink (as a noun) but also to explode (as a verb)

Bust bodice – old English term for a bra; also known as a bust shaper or a bust improver

Buster – an unusually large woman; a giantess

Bustle – a cage like frame designed to be worn under a dress or skirt to give the wearer the appearance of having an exceptionally large bottom

Bustluscious – having shapely breasts

Butt – poor relation, dependent, simpleton (the butt of jokes, wit and ridicule)

Butter upon Bacon – extravagance (the saying comes from the sin of putting butter on the bread when making a bacon sandwich or butty)

Buttered bun – when a man has intercourse with a woman who has just had intercourse with another man the newcomer is said to be enjoying a 'buttered bun'

Buttock and file – shoplifter

Buttock broker – bawd or match maker

Buy my muffins – muffin men used to walk through London's streets at 8 am and 4 pm selling their muffins and crumpets and crying out 'buy my muffins'

Buy your thirst – pay for your own drink

Buxom – lively, good tempered and compliant (and not just well endowed in the bosom department)

Buzzer – motor car, motorised omnibus or, indeed, any vehicle powered by an engine which doesn't run on hay

Byblow – illegitimate child (the word Byblow may come from the word 'bibelot' which is a valuable small object)

By hook or by crook – to get something done, one way or another

By th'good Katty – a Catholic oath which can be used by anyone looking for a suitably inoffensive expletive

C

Cabinet particulier – small private room in a restaurant, where diners could enjoy privacy (the cabinet would possibly include a sofa or bed, presumably in case one or both diners needed a lie down); the phrase was first used in 1859

Cachinnator – someone who laughs loudly and immoderately (cachinnators are popular with those recording TV and radio shows)

Cackle – unconnected string of meaningless words

Cackle-tub – pulpit where a preacher can stand when cackling

Cacophemism – the use of pejorative words or phrases; so for example, the words 'quack' and 'egghead'; cacophemism is the antonym of euphemism

Cads on castors – bicyclists (cyclists were not popular in the 19th century because they were considered to be a hazard to pedestrians; today cyclists seem unpopular with both pedestrians and motorists)

Cake – stupid or foolish man

Calefacient – drug or food that makes you feel warm inside when you swallow it; mid 17th century from the Latin 'calefacient' which means 'making warm'

Calf Round – to ask for something (as a calf does of its mother)

Calicot – snob or cad ('he's an utter calicot')

Callipygian – having shapely buttocks

Camiknickers – a camisole (short bodice) with knickers attached and a flap which buttoned between the legs; camiknickers may be worn over combinations

Camisole – a loose fitting undergarment for the upper body, supported by straps

Camisole bodice – the same as camiknickers

Camp – exaggerated gestures and actions, commonly employed by individuals deficient in character, struggling to draw attention to themselves and whatever it is they are trying to say; the word 'camp' was not originally used to describe those of a homosexual nature

Can you smash a thick 'un – can you break a sovereign ('can I pay with a fifty pound note?')

Canard – false or unfounded rumour; derived from the French word which means 'duck'; the word apparently gained its current usage after a French hoaxer claimed that he had killed one of a score of ducks and fed the remains to the other nineteen, then killing each of the nineteen in turn and feeding them on the meat of the duck he had killed, eventually just leaving one well-fed duck (the sort of story which would have warmed the cockles of Baron Munchausen's heart)

Canary – member of the audience, usually sitting in the gallery, who sings along at a musical (canaries used to be welcomed by performers; these days the police are likely to be called, and performers treated for post-traumatic stress, if a member of the audience dares to do more than hum along quietly)

Candle – as a verb it means to examine minutely (it was common to use a candle when examining an egg to see if it was cracked)

Cant – lies, often based on some religious idea; hypocrisy

Can't see a hole in a forty-foot ladder – too drunk to do anything requiring physical dexterity

Can't you smell the shrimps – can't you smell the sea?

Cantabile – a fairly smooth singing style, from the Italian which means singable

Canterbury story – long, roundabout tale which never seems to reach a climax (derived from Chaucer's 'Canterbury Tales')

Canters – thieves, beggars

Canticle – parish clerk

Canting – preaching with a whining, rather affected tone of voice; maybe a corruption of the word 'chanting' but may also be derived from the memory of a Scottish preacher called Andrew Cant

Cap – captain, sir

Caper merchant – dancing master

Captain Copperthorne's Crew – everyone seems to be an officer; there are too many chiefs and not enough Indians

Captain Queernabs – shabby, ill-dressed fellow

Caravan – large sum of money

Carbuncle – we tend to think of the carbuncle as a large boil or abscess but originally a carbuncle was a precious stone; one of Conan Doyle's best stories for Sherlock Holmes was called 'The Blue Carbuncle' and described how Holmes found a stolen carbuncle in the crop of a fattened Christmas goose (Conan Doyle changed the colour of the carbuncle from its traditional red to blue, but why not – it's called poetic licence)

Carbuncle face – red face full of pimples

Cardigan – sweater with no collar, named after 7th Earl of Cardigan who, when he wasn't designing knitwear, was also the leader of the Charge of the Light Brigade

Carts – a pair of boots, especially a large pair of boots

Cartwheel – a five shilling piece

Case vrow – prostitute attached to a particular bawdy house or brothel

Cassowary – large flightless bird, related to the emu

Cast an optic – take a look at

Castor – hat (early hats were made from beaver skin and beavers are also known as castors so all hats were called 'beavers' or 'castors')

Casualty – black eye (so the music hall song 'Two Lovely Black Eyes' should have been 'Two Lovely Casualties')

Cat – woman (and particularly a quick tempered woman with claws)

Cat heads – breasts (I have no idea who thought this up or why or what was on their mind other than breasts)

Cat on testy dodge – female beggar who goes from house to house, showing a testimonial for a charity and asking for contributions

Cat sticks –thin legs

Cat-sneaking – the stealing of pots from public houses (and, presumably, the re-selling of them to other public houses)

Cat whipping – trick played on ignorant country bumpkins who think they're strong; they are bet that they can be pulled through a pond by a cat; thinking this impossible they accept the bet with delight; a rope is fixed around their waist and the end thrown across the pond; the rope is then tied to the cat with thread; three or four sturdy fellows pretend to whip the cat but pull on the rope, pulling the bumpkin through the water and taking his money

Cataract – an extensive cravat with lots of folds

Catch fart – a servant employed to follow closely behind their master or mistress and, presumably, to 'catch any farts emitted by their master or mistress'; maybe the servant was merely required to take the blame for any gaseous eruptions, particularly noisy or ill-smelling ones

Catch-penny – cheap ballads for which the sheet music was sold in the street (In 1824 a publisher called Catchpin printed a penny ballad called 'We are Alive Again', about a man who was executed for the murder of a fellow called Weare. The sheet of music sold 2,500,000 copies which was pretty good going since this was almost twice the population of London at the time.)

Cater cousins – good friends

Caterpillar – school for ladies (who presumably perambulated through the streets in single file – appearing as a caterpillar)

Caterwauling – going out at night 'in search of intrigues'

Cat's Foot – henpecked man

Cats' Party – gathering of women

Caucus-monger – political agitator

Cauliflower – large, white wig as worn by a clergyman or physician (also the private parts of a woman)

Caulk, Calk – to go to bed to sleep ('Come along children, it's time to caulk.')

Cautions – the four cautions offered to citizens were: 1) beware of a woman in front of you 2) beware of a horse behind you 3) beware of a cart sideways 4) beware of a priest every way

Cavaulting school – bawdy house

Cellars – boots

Chair Days – later years in life; (years which are often mostly spent in a chair)

Chair Warmer – pretty actress who spends her time on stage doing little other than provide decoration

Chamber pot – container kept in the bedroom (usually under the bed – hence sometimes known as a 'guzunder') and used as receptacle for personal waste on cold nights

Champagne shoulders – shoulders which slope, like those of a champagne bottle

Champagne weather – rotten weather (the remark meant sarcastically)

Champion slump of 1897 – the motor car became popular and was regarded as a harbinger of doom

Changeling – a child which, it was believed, had been secretly exchanged by fairies who had taken away the parent's real child; this theory was popular with parents who felt that their ugly, cruel, brutish and stupid child could not possibly be theirs

Chanting-ken – music hall

Chapel – secret meeting of printers, all being members of a trade union

Chappie – pal, chum, mate

Charientism – an elegantly disguised insult, which may not be recognised as such by the target

Charity Bob – rapid, half-hearted curtsey as might be performed by girls attending a charity school as opposed to a decent school where girls were taught to curtsey properly

Charlie Freer – beer (well, it rhymes, which is all that is required of Cockney Rhyming Slang)

Chat – louse

Chatterbox – woman who talks a good deal (the male version is a clackbox)

Chaunter culls – Grub Street writers (hack journalists) who compose songs and ballads and Christmas carols

Chaunting – chanting or singing

Cheeking – being cheeky to someone

Cheese toaster – sword

Chemise – a shirt or blouse like item of clothing

Cheri – lovely, charming woman

Cherubims – peevish children

Cheshire – perfection (as in 'She's the Cheshire', although 'She's the Stilton' was also heard)

Chest and bedding – breasts (name popular with sailors, for some unknown reason)

Chesterfield – a coat, very long and made of white material

Chevy-chase – face (rhyming slang)

Chicken hearted – cowardly

Chin-chin – good health, welcome (originated in Singapore; the proper response is Pa Pa)

Chin-music – proper boxing, involving fighters hitting each other on the jaw

Chin-wag – chatter, natter (the mouth was opening and shutting so the chin was wagging)

Chip – infant or baby (hence 'a chip off the old block')

Chip in – to contribute money to a cause or words to a conversation

Chirrup – to cheer, applaud, usually in a theatre or music hall (artistes were sometimes 'persuaded' to pay out good money in order to be cheered rather than hissed or booed)

Chitterlins – bowels ('I have a rumpus in my chitterlins')

Chitty faced – baby faced

Chiv – knife

Choke off – shut someone up temporarily or permanently

Choker – terminological inexactitude aka a lie

Chopping – large, healthy, handsome child

Chortle – sing or, occasionally, to praise loudly

Chouse – dirty, rotten scoundrel; cheat (derived from the Turkish word 'chaius' since the original 'chouse' meant a crooked Turkish interpreter)

Chrematophobia – fear of money; perhaps the rarest of phobias

Chronic rot –irredeemably awful

Chuck a chest – puff your chest out with pride

Chuck a dummy – faint

Chuck out ink – write an article or news story

Chuck up the bunch of fives – die, abandon life

Chuck up the sponge – admit defeat (from the custom of a boxer's second throwing the sponge into the ring if he feels that his man has taken enough punishment and is not going to win the fight)

Chuckaboo – pal, mate, good friend

Chuckaways – wooden matches, to be thrown away after use

Chuckle – big and clumsy

Chucklehead – stupid person

Chuffy – moody, surly

Chum – close friend (derived, according to Dr Johnson, with whom I do not intend to argue, from the phrase 'a chamber fellow' which refers to university dons and students describing their rooms as chambers, an affectation still adhered to, and also popular with barristers)

Chummage – money paid by richer prisoners in the Fleet and other over-crowded prisons to the poorer prisoners; in return for chummage the richer prisoner would be given a room or cell to themselves and the poorer prisoner would sleep on the stairs (this was known as 'ruffing it')

Chump – head; also a young fool who has been, or is about to be, cheated of his money by a young woman

Church work – any work which proceeds slowly was described as church work; modern motorway repair work could be described as 'church work' as indeed could almost anything involving the law, the civil service and the medical profession

Churched – married

Churchyard cough – deadly chest infection likely to lead to death; the church yard cough was sometimes accompanied by 'cemetery catarrh'

Churl – rude, boorish labourer (gentlemen who drank malt liquor after wine could become 'churlish')

Cigareticide – the bizarre theory that smoking cigarettes was a dangerous habit was known as cigareticide and was first aired in 1883, though it was dismissed as utter nonsense by the medical establishment which, as it nearly always does, acted in its own financial interests rather than in the interests of patients

Cinder garbler – servant maid who sifts ashes from cinders

Cinder-sifter – type of bowler hat with a very upturned brim

Cinderella – dance which ends at midnight

Circumforaneous – wandering from place to place and house to house; as used to be practised by political candidates, women selling cosmetics and salesmen selling brushes

Circumlocution – to use more words than are necessary

Cit – citizen of London

Civility money – fee charged by bailiffs for conducting their affairs with civility

Clackbox – male chatterbox

Claim – to recognise someone while out and about (as in 'I claim you, don't I?')

Clap – venereal disease (someone with a venereal disease was said to have gone out by Had'em and come home by Clapham)

Clap on the shoulder – to be arrested for debt

Clapperdogeon – a born beggar

Clatterfart – gossip; first used in 1552 though I don't know by whom

Clean tuckered out – knackered

Clear – very drunk

Cleavage – the hollow between a woman's breasts; the breasts usually being supported by a special undergarment and exposed by a low cut dress or other garment

Clergyman's daughter – prostitute (amateur or professional)

Clerisy – literary folk, regarded as members of a social group

Clicker – salesman's servant or someone in a gang who shares out the booty among the rest of the thieves

Clicket – copulation ('the cull and the mort are at clicket in the dyke' means the man and the woman are copulating in the ditch)

Clickman toad – watch; this strange phrase originated when a West country man who had never seen a watch found on a heath and, by the shape and the motion of the hand and the noise of the wheels, he concluded it was a living creature of the toad kind and because it made a clicking noise he called it a 'clickman toad' (incidentally, the reference to 'the hand' rather than 'the hands' is not an error, early watches and clocks had one hand, since that provided all the required information (we have a 17th century long case clock in our hallway which has just one hand and has managed perfectly well in that state for around 400 years)

Cloak twitchers – rogues who hang around the entrances to dark alleys in order to snatch cloaks from the shoulders of people passing by

Clobbered – well-nourished and well dressed

Clod hopper – country farmer

Close – in the 18th century dictionary 'Blackguardiana', the word 'close was defined as 'close as God's curse to a whore's arse'. However, although being colourful this explanation obviously doesn't take us very much further forward.

Clout – blow ('I'll give you a clout on your jolly nob' means 'I'll hit you on the head'); however, a clout was also a handkerchief so 'I'll give you a clout on your jolly nob' could also mean 'I'll put a handkerchief on your head')

Cloven – a woman who passes as a maiden but isn't one

Cloven inlet – vagina and environs

Clover – to live in clover is to live in luxury

Club –meeting or association, usually where each man was expected to pay the same sum of money to enter

Clump – stupid lump of a person

Clunch – awkward, clownish fellow

Clutter – noise or racket

Cly faking – picking a pocket and taking the contents – particularly a handkerchief

Clyster pipe – apothecary

Coach wheel – half a crown

Coal up – feed

Coax – fondle or wheedle; also used to mean to darn as in 'I've coaxed your socks'

Cob – punishment used by sailors among themselves; it involves 'bastinadoing the offender on the posterior with a cobbing stick or pipe staff'; this was done a dozen times with all those present removing their hats at the start of the punishment; the last stroke had to be given as hard as possible and it was called 'a purse'

Cock alley – if you have to ask what this means then you aren't old enough to know

Cock a whoop – elated

Cock and bull story – roundabout story without a beginning or an end

Cock bawd – man running a brothel or bawdy house

Cock catching – obtaining money by craftiness; confidence trickery

Cock lane – same as cock alley

Cock of the walk – leader

Cock pimp – husband of a bawd

Cockalorum – little man with a high opinion of himself

Cockish – wanton

Cockney – citizens of London born within the sound of Bow Bell; the story behind this is that a Londoner from that part of the city heard a horse neigh for the first time and cried out 'Lord, how that horse laughs'; a bystander told him the noise was called 'neighing'; the next morning the Londoner heard a cock crow and to show that he had remembered the word he'd been taught, cried out 'Do you hear how the cock neighs'

Cocks – medicines and concoctions of some or no value available from a dispensing chemist

Cockshut time – when fowls go to roost

Cocotte – young woman, traditionally French, who sells her virtue, usually at a high price

Cod – as a noun this means a fool, as a verb it means to trick or cheat, sometimes through flattery

Cod-bangers – well-dressed fishermen who, having sold their catch spend their money on fine clothes

Codger – older male person, and, generally speaking, one who usually enjoys a good time, although the word is often used disparagingly as though the elderly are unpleasant, bad tempered and mean

Codshead – stupid person; someone with the brain of a fish

Codswallop – nonsense (possibly named after Hiram Codd who is remembered for having invented a bottle for fizzy drinks in 1875)

Coffee-sisters – women who meet for coffee and to share gossip (biscuits and cake are optional)

Cog – to cheat at dice; also to coax or wheedle money or refreshment out of someone ('to cog a dinner' means to cadge a free meal)

Coker-nuts – unusually well-developed breasts (see also 'prize faggots' and please remember I didn't make this stuff up but am merely reporting the language that was used over 100 years ago by people who didn't know any better and didn't have radio, television or social media to keep themselves busy)

Cold burning – punishment inflicted on soldiers on their comrades for trifling offences; the prisoner was put against a wall with an arm held high above his head; the 'executioner' then stood on a stool and poured cold water down the soldier's sleeve until it ran out of his breeches; if the soldier had been punished to be 'burned' in both arms then the procedure was repeated for the other arm. One assumes that this punishment was later adopted and refined by the Central Intelligence Agency.

Cold Cook – undertaker

Cold Day – rotten luck

Cold Meat – dead body

College – workhouse or prison ('My family is away at college' or 'My Uncle Tom is spending three years at college')

Collie shangels – rows, arguments, quarrels (originated in Scotland and brought South by no less a linguist than Queen Victoria in her journal entitled 'More Leaves' in 1884)

Comb and Brush – lush, someone who drinks alcohol with rather too much enthusiasm

Combinations – a camisole attached to a pair of drawers; they were sometimes provided with a slit between legs and one at back to enable the wearer to visit the lavatory without undressing entirely; combinations were popular in Victorian times when the layers of clothing meant that going to the lavatory must have been a complex and time consuming procedure for a lady.

Come and have a pickle – invitation to a snack

Come and wash your neck – invitation to have a drink

Come-down – humiliation, embarrassment and ruin ('they sold their hansom cab and bought a gig, what a come down')

Come in – becoming trendy or fashionable ('You mark my words, brown Victorian furniture will come in one of these days')

Come out – appear in society, to be received and even accepted by posh people

Come the old soldier – to approach a possible benefactor and ask for money. (The Duke of Wellington was constantly pestered by men who claimed to be old soldiers who had served under him and who were in need of a square meal or a libation.)

Comiconomenclaturist – someone who enjoys collecting funny names, of which there are many

Comstockism – prudery, specifically objecting to the painting of women without clothes. Comstock was an American who campaigned constantly against nudity in art. He was reputed to turn out the light when taking a bath.

Concatanation – collection of circumstances

Condom – prophylactic, named after an 18th century English physician and military man called Dr Condom; early condoms were made of tortoiseshell, which must have been fun for all concerned though later condoms were made from the dried gut of a sheep; there is some dispute about how the inventor spelt his name and some ancient dictionaries describe him as Colonel Cundum; extra added confusion is offered by the fact that a cundum is also a scabbard for a sword and an oil skin case for holding the regimental colours

Confidence-queen – female detective (Miss Marple was, therefore, a Confidence-queen.)

Conspiracy of Silence – politicians and publishers avoiding controversial issues (the phrase was first used in 1885)

Cook ruffian – bad cook

Cooking with gas – if someone remarks that they are 'cooking with gas' they are suggesting that things are going exceptionally well

Cool lady – camp follower who sells brandy to soldiers

Cool tankard – wine and water with lemon, sugar and burrage

Collector – highwayman

Collegiates – prisoners (no one went to prison because prisons were known as colleges)

Colt – young man apprenticed to roguery

Comb – to scold; a woman who lectures her husband is said to 'comb his head'; the word 'comb' was sometimes extended in meaning, so 'she combed his head with a stool' means 'she threw a stool at his head'

Commodity – a woman's commodity is defined as 'the private parts of a lady' and 'the public parts of a prostitute'

Conger – when one bookseller buys a good copy of a book and other booksellers are allowed to make as many copies as they like at stated prices – that's a conger

Conny wabble – eggs and brandy beaten together

Content – liquid made with milk and gingerbread to look a bit like chocolate

Conundrum – enigmatic conceit

Cop – suffer a defeat of some kind (to be 'copped' was to be caught)

Cop a mouse – suffer a black eye

Copper – policeman (the word followed on from Bobby and Peeler as those terms became unfashionable)

Copper-clawing – women fighting

Copper's shanty – police station

Copper-slosher – someone who has a habit of attacking coppers

Coquettish – wanton at worst, flirtatious at best; 17th century word from 'coq'

Cordwood – wood chopped into lengths suitable for building a house, making a fence or burning in a hearth

Corinthian – originally belonging to Corinth and Corinthian architecture, but later used to denote a high standard of amateur sportsmanship, often suggesting a sportsman with a portfolio of skills; the word was also used to describe as someone who frequents brothels

Corner Boys – youths and men who stand on street corners doing nothing very much; loafers

Corny face – pimpled features

Corporal – to mount a corporal and four is a euphemism for masturbation; the thumb is the corporal and the four fingers are the privates

Corporation – large belly

Corpse – an actor on stage who is not speaking but nevertheless uses mannerisms or actions to attract the attention of the audience is 'corpsing'. (These days actors who suddenly start laughing inappropriately are said to have corpsed. The late Peter Sellers did it a great deal and directors are reputed to have added a few days to their shooting schedules to allow for his corpsing.)

Corsair – privateer or pirate; particularly one operating in the southern Mediterranean during the 17th century

Corselet – a piece of armour which covered the trunk (from late 15th century); later the word came to describe a foundation garment which consists of a corset and a bra (the spelling slowly changed to corselette); there are two main types of corselette – the version which incorporates a pair of panties and the version which is open at the lower end and which is usually fitted with suspenders to hold up stockings

Corset – tight fitting undergarment, strong enough to shape the figure from bust to hips; traditionally a corset began under the bust though modern corsets include support for the bosom; corsets are worn by both men and women to support a weak or injured back; the word is Middle English from Old French

Corset cover – an item which, in Victorian times (when ladies wore numerous layers of clothing), was worn over the corset

Coruscate – to sparkle or glitter; early 18th century from Latin verb 'coruscare'

Coryza – medical term for a runny nose or common cold; in use from the early 16th century

Cosey – small cosy pub where the patrons could (or can) be found drinking, singing, dancing and, generally, having a good time at any time of day

Cotquean – a man doing a woman's work and having feminine concerns

Cotswold lion – sheep

Couch a hogshead – lie down to sleep

Cough drop – anything disagreeable but particularly a poison

Counterfeit crank – a cheat; especially one who pretends to be ill when he (or she) isn't

Country put – ignorant country fellow

Courtesan – women who make a profession out of prostitution; in the year 1800, London was estimated to contain 50,000 prostitutes, not counting those operating privately or as mistresses; courtesans, probably regarded as those at the head of their profession, could earn huge sums (£10,000 or so) for a single night's work

Cove – man, probably a rogue

Covent Garden ague – venereal disease

Covent Garden nun – prostitute

Coventry – army officers guilty of improper behaviour, but nothing serious enough for a court martial, were sent to Coventry – i.e. they were ignored completely; when it was decided that the punishment could end, the unfortunate soul would be welcomed back as though he had just returned from a journey to Coventry

Covey – collection of whores (the accepted collective term)

Cow handed – awkward

Cow hearted – frightened, cowardly

Cowcumbers to pickle – was a street cry heard for centuries from the days of Queen Elizabeth I; in the late 18th century, street traders would sell cucumbers at a penny for twelve

Cow-juice – milk

Cowlick – a wisp of hair looking different to all other hairs on a head (lick is a bastardisation of lock, and where the cow came into this has been a mystery to lexicographers for as long as there have been dictionaries)

Coxcomb – a fool but a vain and conceited fool; taken in the 16th century from the cap worn by a court jester, which was called cockscomb

Crack a case – break into a house in order to steal ('case' is taken from casa – the Italian for house)

Crack the monica – ring a bell (the 'monica' was the bell rung by the chairman at music halls when variety acts were appearing)

Cracker – backside; breeches were known as farting-crackers

Crackpot – swindler, confidence trickster, crooked company promoter (a crackpot might sell a patent medicine or a gold mine with no gold in it)

Cranky gawk – awkward, rather stupid youth not much good for anything

Crapulence – relating to drinking and drunkenness in all its variegated forms

Cramp words – sentence of death spoken by a judge (presumably because the prisoner being sentenced feels abdominal cramps – and who wouldn't?)

Crap – money

Crapper – flush toilet, named after its creator Thomas Crapper (hence the verb 'to crap')

Crapulous – to feel ill, usually having had too much to eat or drink, hungover ('It was a good party last night, I feel positively crapulous today.')

Crave a boon – to make a special request

Craw thumper – Roman Catholic, thus called because of their believed habit of beating their breasts when confessing their sins (Catholics were also known as a brisket beater)

Cream pot love – when a young man flirts with a dairy maid in order to get hold of cream and other tasty products

Cremorne – open air space (such as public gardens) patronised by women of doubtful virtue (There once was a garden of that name where there were reputed to be more women of doubtful virtue than flowers.)

Crew – gang (male criminals, rascals and rogues were known as abrams, frathers, priggers of prancers, upright men, rufflers, dummerers, jarkmen, patricoes, pedlars, swadders and tinkers while female criminal were called bawdy baskets, morts, doxies, delles and kinching coes)

Cribbage faced – marked with the small pox scars, so called because the scars were said to bear some resemblance to the holes in a cribbage board

Crim con money – damages ordered by a jury to be paid by an adulterer to the injured husband for having had 'criminal conversation with his wife'

Crinkum – venereal disease

Crinkum-crankum – word of contempt for over-decorated things; architecture with unnecessary knobs on and the collected debris which fills living rooms with, it seems, the sole purpose of collecting dust; became a rather contemptuous word for fussy, over decorated things and was therefore a word exceedingly well used in Victorian times; also sometimes used, rather strangely, as a euphemism for the vagina and surroundings and this doubtless led to some confusion from time to time

Crinoline – stiffened or hooped petticoat draped over bell shaped cage and often quilted with horsehair; the idea was to make a skirt stick out but the snag was that if a woman wearing a crinoline leant too far forward she would display to those behind her more than was, at the time, considered proper. Moreover, a gust of wind could also endanger the wearer's modesty by lifting the entire structure into the air

Crinoline cage – the metal cage over which was worn layers of petticoats and a dress

Crispin's holiday – every Monday is Crispin's holiday

Croak – hypocritical

Crock – bicycle

Cropsick – stomach sickness caused by drinking too much alcohol

Cross-grained – difficult person (taken from the fact that cross-grained wood is difficult to use)

Cross patch – peevish person, usually a boy or girl

Crotchetty – unpredictable, unexpected and rather odd

Crowbar Brigade – Irish policemen who had a reputation for using crowbars to remove tenants from properties were known as members of the crowbar brigade

Crow's nest – attic bedroom in country house, a room usually given to a visiting bachelor who was not considered particularly significant

Crum-a-grackle – a puzzle, an awkward situation, a difficulty

Crump – someone who helps solicitors serve affidavits or provide false witnesses

Crump backed – hump backed

Crumpet – round cake intended to be toasted and buttered and bearing more than a passing resemblance to the English muffin (from the 17th century); later (from the 1930s) crumpet became a word describing women, especially if considered a suitable object of sexual desire (in this respect the word 'crumpet' was a favourite of the late racing driver Stirling Moss who would dismiss comments comparing his relatively low earning capacity (when compared to the drivers of the 21st century) by remarking that he and his colleagues 'had the crumpet, boy')

Crush the stur – break out of prison

Crushed – be in love with someone

Crusty beau – man who uses paint and cosmetics to improve his appearance

Crusty fellow – surly fellow

Cryptorchid – condition in which one or both testicles have failed to descend into the scrotum; first appeared in use in the late 19th century

Cub – ill educated young man, still finding his way in the world

Cuckold – husband of an incontinent wife. 'To cuckold the parson' meant to sleep with one's bride-to-be before marriage

Cuff – old man

Cuff-shooter – clerk in an office; moving the arm to push forward shirt cuffs was known as cuff shooting

Culver-head – idiot

Cumbrous – cumbersome (a word used largely by poets for its superior rhyming quality)

Cunning shaver – a sharp fellow who is clever at cheating

Cunny warren – girls' boarding school

Cunnyborough – vagina and environs

Cup o'tea – comfort, consolation (the thought was often accompanied by the reality)

Cupboard love – making love to the cook (or flirting with her) in order to obtain a free meal

Cupid's kettledrums – breasts

Curbing Law – using a hook to steal goods out of a window (the curb is the hook and the curber is the thief)

Curds and whey – in the 18th century, milk and cream sellers, usually Welsh or Irish girls, sold cream at one shilling and four-pence a pint and sold milk at four-pence a quart

Curfew – bedtime, cover the fire (from the French 'couvre-fue'); in the 11th century William Conqueror decided that all fires had to be extinguished by 8 pm, making it too cold to watch television in the winter evenings and resulting in a boost to the size of the population

Curmudgeon – surly or bad tempered person, invariably male, constantly ready to find fault with the world (originated in 17th century France with the phrase 'coeur mechant')

Curmuring – low rumbling sound in the bowels

Curtain lecture – a woman who scolds her husband when in bed is said to be reading him a curtain lecture

Cushion – when a woman has a boy, the husband can rest (on a cushion) since 'he has done his business'

Cut – drunk

Cut a finger – to release odiferous intestinal gases (heaven may know why a smelly fart should be described as a cut finger but no one on earth seems to know though doubtless a PhD student bereft of more useful ideas will one day make this puzzle his life's work; in spiritual terms a cut finger is said to be a sign that change is necessary though I would venture to suggest that a cut finger may also be a result of the finger's owner being careless with a sharp knife)

Cut and run – to depart without warning or permission (probably derived from the habit of sailors leaving a port in the middle of the night to escape debts – they would cut the mooring ropes and run with the wind)

Cut the line – knock off work for a while (originated with printers who used to set lines of print)

Cycling fringe – hairstyle popular with lady cyclists

Cyrano – large nose (from the hero of Cyrano de Bergerac who had a larger than average sized proboscis)

D

Dab – adept at something (a dab hand); an alternative, surprising definition is that a dab occurs 'when a man hits his wife on the arse with a pound of butter' though I can find no explanation for this usage which does appear in respectable sources

Daddles – hands; 'give me your daddle' means 'give me your hand'

Dag – wool and shit hanging off the rear of a sheep

Daisy – a charming person or thing might be referred to as a 'daisy'

Daisy-five-o'clocker – a lovely five o'clock tea

Daisy kickers – ostlers at great inns

Damager – manager

Damfino – a short version of 'I am damned if I know'

Damme boy – blustering fellow; a 'kicker up of a breeze'

Damp bourbon poultice – a glass of whiskey

Damper – luncheon or snap before dinner; likely to dampen the appetite

Dance upon nothing – to be hanged (a hanged person's legs will twitch in a manner vaguely reminiscent of dancing)

Dander – a show of temper, scurf or a cinder; few words have, over the years, collected as many different meanings; dander can also mean a gentle stroll, a wander

Dandiprat – anything small; not necessarily beautiful; the word began life meaning a small coin and ended up meaning a small boy

Dangle – to follow a woman

Dangler – man who follows women without knowing them; also someone hanging or about to be hung

Daphlean – shy and beautiful

Dark as a pocket – very dark indeed

Dark cully – married man who keeps a mistress whom he visits only at night

Darkman's budge – someone who slides into a house in the dark and hides, so as later to let in a gang to rob the place

David Jones – the spirit of the sea

David's sow – 'as drunk as David's sow' was a common phrase in the 17th and 18th centuries; a Welshman called David Lloyd kept a pub at Hereford and had a sow with six legs which was often viewed by curious visitors; Mr Lloyd also had a wife who drank too much and for which he 'sometimes gave her due correction'; one day, while drunk, Mrs Lloyd turned the sow out of its sty and lay down to sleep in its place; when a party of visitors came to see the sow, Mr Lloyd ushered them in the direction of the sty and, without looking, said: 'There is a sow for you. Did you ever see such another?' The visitors, seeing the drunken woman, agreed that it was the drunkenest sow they had ever seen. Thereafter Mrs Lloyd was known as David's sow.

Davy – affadavit

Dawb – bribe; also to decorate

Dead cargo – phrase used by thieves who are disappointed in their stolen booty

Dead men – empty bottles

Deadly – the gallows, also known as the 'three legged mare'

Dear old thing – often over-used greeting, usually preceded by 'My' as in 'My dear old thing'; first used in 1852

Death hunter – undertaker who sells specialist clothing etc., required for funerals

Death promoter – alcohol (the danger of alcohol in excess has been recognised for a long time)

Decencies – padding used by male actors to cover and disguise (and possibly enhance) nature's endowments

Decoction – concentrated liquid; a soup or a medicine; like so many words in this book 'decoction is an old word from Middle English'

Decolletage – a low neckline on a woman's dress or blouse, sometimes offering a view of the woman's cleavage. In 17th century France more than amply built ladies used the area below their decolletage as a storage area for holding a handkerchief, a purse, and letters. The amount of storage space depended on the size of the cleavage which depended, of course, upon the size of the breasts

Defenstration – throwing someone out of a window; early 17th word from the Latin de = down and fenestra = window

Deipnosophist – someone skilled in making dinner table conversation; deipnosophobia is a more modern word describing a condition in which an individual is frightened of having to make conversation at a dinner party

Dells – buxom young wenches who were virgins; dells who found themselves in a gang would have their virginity taken by the gang's 'upright man' and only then be made free for the rest of the fraternity (when they would become common strumpets)

Delo nammow – old woman

Demergature – death by drowning; more specifically, and on occasion, suicide by drowning

Demi-lass – a polite word for trollop, slut or slag

Demirep (or demy rep) – someone with no reputation at all or, at least, not a reputation to be envied

Derby – to pawn (comes from the habit of men pawning their watches to raise money to bet on the Derby horse race); the word is also used to describe a type of hat and a specific horse race (both these were named after the 12th Earl of Derby)

Derick – a tower with a hoist, named after Goodman Derick who was an English hangman in the early 17th century

Desuetude – a state of disuse

Devil – printer's errand boy

Devil catcher – parson

Devil's dinner hour – midnight

Devil's guts – a surveyor's chain, disliked by farmers who didn't like to have their land measured, fearing, no doubt with sound reasoning, that no good could come of it

Devil's luck and my own – no damned luck at all

Devils on horseback – prunes, wrapped in bacon, cooked and served on toast

Devonshire compliment – comment which appears polite but which is rather doubtful

Dewitted – torn to pieces by the mob

Dewlaps – a fold of loose skin at the throat (cf wattle)

Diddeys – breasts

Diddle – gin

Dildo – in the late 16th century a dildo was described as 'an implement resembling the virile member, for which it is said to be substituted by nuns, boarding school misses and others obliged to celibacy or fearful of pregnancy'. Dildoes were reputedly made of wax, horn, leather and 'diverse other substances' and were sold at 'many of our great toyshops and nick nackatories'.

Dimber – pretty

Dimber damber – top man

Ding boy – rogue, bully or card sharper

Dingle – wooded valley or dell; originally derived from Middle English but the current use dates only from the 17th century so is quite recent and can be considered to be just settling into the language

Dipped in the Shannon – impudent (usually about an impudent Irishman)

Directoire knickers – long knickers gathered at the waist and round the leg, fastened with buttons or elastic (favoured by upper class French women during the French Directory period of late 18th century and subsequently adopted by upper class English women)

Dirty puzzle – nasty slut

Discalceate – shoeless; originally used to describe friars and nuns who wore sandals rather than shoes it is sometimes used to describe individuals who are barefoot; the word is derived from 'calceus' which is, as we all know, Latin for shoe

Diseuse – female artiste who entertained with monologues

Discombobulated – confused or disconcerted; from the mid 19th century

Disguised – drunk

Dish of rails – scolding (usually from a disgruntled wife)

Dishclout – a dirty, greasy woman; a man who made a napkin of his dishclout was a man who married his cook or maid; female servants in a kitchen would often threaten to pin a dishclout to a man's tail if he pried too minutely into the secrets of the kitchen

Ditch – the Atlantic Ocean

Dithyramb – passionate writing, either as an essay or poem

Diver – pickpocket (from diving his hand into other people's pockets)

Divide – divide the house with one's wife; to give her the outside and keep the inside (therefore turning her out into the street)

Divided drawers – a pair of legs attached separately to a waistband with straps; divided drawers were sometimes made of old flour sacks with the result that the wearer might well appear to have the words 'Peacock's aerated pastry flour 28 lb' stamped on her bottom, though this would not, of course, be visible to the casual observer

Dizzy age – old age ('he's reached the dizzy age' of 42)

Do him a treat – give him a thrashing

Do oneself well – try to succeed

Doctor – milk and water with rum and nutmeg

Doctor Brighton – Brighton had a reputation as a health-giving resort (it is said that it was George IV who first referred to Brighton as Doctor Brighton; courtiers, as creepy then as they are now, no doubt chuckled appreciatively and may have clapped a little at the King's witticism)

Doctor Jim – soft felt hat with a wide brim, rather like a Fedora

Doctors – loaded dice; 'they put the doctors upon him' means they cheated him with loaded dice

Dog – clever, cheery man

Dog cheap – unbelievably cheap (Dryden described a group of harlots as 'dog cheap')

Dog Latin – barbarous Latin as used by lawyers and doctors

Dog's legs – chevron worn by non-commissioned officers such as corporals and sergeants

Dog's portion – a lick and a smell (said about a dangler after women who is not very successful)

Dog's soup – rain water

Doggie – batman or officer's servant

Doily – small, entirely pointless mat made of lace or paper, usually placed on a plate, with sandwiches or cakes placed on the doily; the doily was devised by a London draper called Mr Doyley

Doing the bear – courting which involves hugging (a young girl might report that her young man was doing the bear to her)

Doliochocnemic – having long legs

Doliochoproscopic – having a long and narrow face

Doll – tawdry, overdressed woman who looks a bit like a doll

Dollars to buttons – a sure bet

Dolly – contrivance for washing clothes, consists of a wheel in a tub which when filled with soap and water and the wheel turned washes linen; when I became an Agony Uncle for a national newspaper my first letter was from a woman wanting to know where she could obtain 'dolly blue', a special type of soap for this device

Dolly mop –overdressed servant girl; also a prostitute

Donnybrook – noisy disturbance, bordering on a riot

Don't sell me a dog – don't cheat me (from the idea that dog dealers are thieves)

Doodle – a filthy fellow, a noodle

Dook – large nose (obviously derived from the Duke of Wellington who was exceptionally well equipped in that area)

Door mat – big beard, often untrimmed

Dorsay – perfect (originated with the Count d'Orsay, he of the railway station and museum, who was considered perfect)

Double-plated blow-hard – bull-shitter, boaster

Dowdying – a popular practical joke in the town of Salisbury in England, which was played on groups of people, and particularly on those who had boasted of their courage. A man called Pearce, who had the ability to impersonate madness, would burst into a room as though he had just escaped from his keeper, terrifying everyone not in on the secret. Pearce was known as Dowdy because he used to sing a song for which the words were 'dow de dow'.

Doxies – women who have somehow contrived to be neither married nor virginal

Drab – nasty, sluttish whore

Drag – skirt or petticoat worn by an actor playing a female part on stage (so named because a skirt would drag on the stage in a way that a pair of trousers would not)

Drapery Miss – pretty, high born, fashionable young female who has a large wardrobe which will, she hopes, be paid for when she is married (according to Lord Byron, writing in Don Juan)

Drawers – knickers which were long enough to cover the thigh and upper part of the lower leg, popular in Victorian times; before that time drawers meant stockings

Drawlatch – robber of those houses where the doors were closed only with latches

Dress – to beat or bash

Dromedary – big, heavy thief

Drop – lose money, as in 'I dropped fifty guineas on the horses today'

Drop a cog – the conman would drop a piece of gold or silver in a place where he and a passer-by would both see it; the conman would pick up the gold or silver (in reality gold plated base metal) and then bargain with the passer by (suggesting that the passer-by keep the coin or ring and pay him a small amount of money). This trick is still commonly played in Paris and in the early years of the 21st century it was difficult to walk for more than half an hour in the city, along quiet streets, without being confronted by someone trying the trick.

Drum – cell or house

Drumbelo – dull, heavy fellow

Drury Lane Ague – venereal disease, possibly caught from a Drury Lane Vestal (see below)

Drury Lane Vestal – prostitute, particularly one working in the area around London's Drury Lane

Dry bob – smart repartee; and also copulation without ejaculation

Dry boots – humorous fellow

Duchess – woman who is made love to by a man with his boots still on, or while still wearing her own shoes, is a 'duchess'; the word has also long been used as a synonym for 'mother'

Duddering rake – lewd rake, a buck

Dude – cool, stylish, confident man; possibly a bit of a dandy

Duff – not very good; multipurpose exclamatory word as in 'He is the most duffing duffer that ever duffed'. Curiously it also means pregnant as in 'up the duff'.

Duffers – confidence tricksters who pretend to deal in smuggled goods. The trickster would offer items to country folk visiting the city and suggest that the price was low because the items had been smuggled into the country. In fact, of course, the goods had been bought locally and were sold at twice their worth.

Dugs – breasts

Duke Humphrey – to dine with Duke Humphrey was to fast (a Duke of Gloucester called Humphrey was famous for frequent fasting)

Dumb glutton – woman's private parts

Dummerer – someone who pretends to be dumb

Dumpling – short, chubby man or woman

Dun – to demand money; the word originated with a bailiff in the town of Lincoln whose name was Joe Dun and who had a reputation for being aggressive

Dunce – a bit of an idiot – named after a 13th century Scottish theologian called John Duns Scotus (poor Mr Scotus wasn't all that dim but his followers were)

Dunghill – coward

Dust – light touch

Dustman – dead man

Dutch concert – musical event where everyone plays or sings a different tune

Dutch feast – a dinner where the host gets drunk before his guests

Dying duck in a thunderstorm (like a...) – looking miserable, dejected, hopeless, disappointed; from late 18th century

Dyspepsia – madness brought on by drink

E

Earnest – to bind a bargain by paying a deposit in part payment

Easy – to gag or kill a cull or a victim is to 'easy' him

Eat vinegar with a fork – set on edge

Ecdysiast –originally a snake sloughing its skin but, more recently, a strip tease practitioner

Eenque – queen (Victorians liked messing around with words)

Eesome – someone or something considered pleasing to the eye

Elbow grease – hard work

Eldritch – sinister, ghostly, weird (an early 16th century word which was originally from Scotland)

Eleemosynary – dependent on charity (from the late 16th century)

Elephant's trunk – drunk (another silly bit of Cockney rhyming slang)

Elevator – crinolette; a crinoline projecting backwards to make the posterior more obvious; the whole thing would be decorated with a bow designed to draw even more attention to the woman's bottom

Elf – small man or woman

Emboinpoint – technically this noun describes plumpness but it is usually used to describe the area above the waist in a woman and is therefore more accurately defined as 'a woman's bosom'

Embranglement – a tangle of argument and abuse

Endacotted – illegally arrested (the word was sometimes reduced to 'cotted')

Ender – second rate music hall artist who went on stage towards the end of an evening's entertainment, just as the audience was leaving

English burgundy – porter

Entire squat – household, including wife, children and servants

Epicene – androgynous; having both male and female characteristics and/or being of indeterminate sex

Ergophobia – fear of work or an aversion to work, a fear of finding a job or being forced to take a job or a fear of a particular task associated with a job (always common, now an epidemic)

Esculent – something edible

Establish a funk – make a panic

Esurient – hungry or generally having a greedy nature

Eternity box – coffin

Ethnic – a population subgroup within a larger national or cultural group; and so it can be said that English heterosexuals (of both sexes) are members of an ethnic group in Britain

Ethnocentric – looking at all other cultures in comparison with your own culture and making judgements; ethnocentric individuals tend to assume that their own culture is superior to all other cultures

Etui – needle case or small case for toilet articles; a popular alternative to bath salts and socks as a Christmas gift

Evanescent – quickly forgotten, leaving only a quickly fading impression

Evening wheeze – false news designed to sell evening newspapers; this has been extended and is a 24 hour a day wheeze, with television companies and websites creating false news on an hourly basis

Everlasting knock – death

Everything is nice in your garden – commonly said to the self-satisfied and boastful (alleged to have been said in earnest by Queen Victoria to a daughter of Princess Beatrice who was rather pleased with her own little patch of garden but then used in a sarcastic sense by millions)

Ewe – a white ewe is a beautiful woman; an old ewe dressed as lamb is an old woman dressed like a girl

Exoptable – very desirable

Expostulate – to disagree or disapprove of someone very much and, as a result, to argue earnestly

Extra – a performer on stage who doesn't speak, dance or sing but is just there. Most extras in 19th century theatre shows were pretty girls with no talent but a yearning to appear on the stage (and possibly to attract the attention of a gentleman looking for a dinner companion)

Eye sore – ugly or disagreeable object

F

Fabulist – liar; technically suggests someone who makes up fables (or tells them) but since the word is little known it can be used with more impunity than the word 'liar'; to be fair a fabulist is defined as someone who invents elaborate but dishonest stories (as per Baron Munchhausen) rather than someone who fibs about where he/she was on Tuesday evening; the word 'fabulist' is late 16th century and derived from the Latin word fabula which means fable

Face making – to beget children; to face it out (to persist in a falsity); to bluff at cards

Face the music – meet difficulties head-on without trying to evade them

Face ticket – to be so well recognised when entering a place requiring an admission ticket that the admission ticket isn't required and the commissionaires will nod you through (first used about regulars at the British Museum)

Facer – glass filled to the brim

Facinorous – extremely wicked

Fade – shabby dude or masher

Fadge – it won't fadge means it just won't do

Fag – to beat; as a noun it means a boy who acts as a servant for another

Fagger – small boy put through a window to rob a house

Faineant – idle or useless person

Fair trod on – ill used

Fairy – debauched, drunken old woman

Fairy belt – a belt, popular in Victorian times, which was worn to give a woman the appearance of having a narrow, wasp-like waist

Fake pie – pie made at the end of the week and filled with all sorts of unwanted left overs

Fallalls – ornaments such as ribbons or necklaces; fancy lingerie designed to be seen rather than to keep the wearer warm

Famgrasp – shake hands

Fan – to beat

Fandangle – something useless and purely ornamental at best; first used in the 19th century

Fanning the hammer – an unscrupulous action; the phrase is derived from the habit of gunslingers in America wiring back the trigger of a gun so that they could shoot faster; the gun is held in the left hand and the edge of the right hand is used to 'fan' or strike the hammer so all the bullets fly out very quickly

Fart catcher – a valet or footman who walks behind his or her master

Farthing faced chit – as insignificant as a farthing

Farthing-taster – very small quantity of very cheap ice cream

Farouche – sullen or sly in company

Farthingale – wooden or padded structure attached to the waist in order to extend the hips sideways. Because a farthingale sometimes carried a huge skirt of up to 11 feet wide, the structure had to be lowered with a piece of string to enable the wearer to pass through doorways.

Fat cull – rich man

Fat headed – stupid

Faulkner – tumbler, magician or juggler

Fauteuil – wooden armchair with upholstered arms but open sides

Feather bed lane – rough or stony lane

Feather in her mouth – about to lose her temper ('watch out – she has a feather in her mouth')

Feel cheap – humiliated

Fellow commoner – empty bottle

Felts – hats, of various styles (men removed them when meeting someone or entering a house but once a woman put on a hat she kept it on)

Female personator – man dressed in feminine clothing and singing and dancing while pretending to be female (believe it or not, a male personator was a woman dressed in masculine clothing and singing and dancing while pretending to be male)

Fen – common prostitute (there were a good many words for prostitutes in the 17th and 18th centuries, but there were a good many prostitutes)

Ferrara – the name of a famous sword maker who specialised in double edged broad swords or claymores as used by Scottish Highlanders (the word is early 18th century)

Ferret – tradesman who sells goods to young heirs who have little or no ready money but charges them extortionate interest rates and then duns them heavily for the debt

Fettle – in the South of England, fettle usually means condition and is invariably accompanied by the word as in 'fine fettle'; in the North of England, however, fettle is a verb meaning to mend, repair or even tinker with and so a cobbler might professionally fettle a flapping sole while today an amateur motor cycle mechanic might fettle his bike's engine on the kitchen table, doubtless much to the delight of his wife (the word is Old English)

Fib – to beat or rob, as well as to lie

Fiddle faddle – nonsense

Field Lane duck – baked bullock's heart. (Field Lane was near to Saffron Hill, where Fagin, a character from Charles Dickens' book 'Oliver Twist' would have hung out if he had been real)

Field running – building rubbishy houses on suburban fields (these days most of the suburban fields have been built on and so builders, aided and abetted by planning authorities, put their rickety houses on flood plains so that they can flood while they are falling down)

Fifteen puzzle – confusion; the Fifteen puzzle consisted of moveable cubes, upon each of which was a number. The aim was to arrange the cubes in a square so that every line added up to fifteen. The puzzle, which was introduced in 1879, was incredibly popular

Fighting the tiger – gambling

Filch – beggar's staff which has a hook at the end so that it could be used to steal items through a window

Filchman – truncheon carried by rogues

File – pickpocket; a pickpocket would often work with a man called a bulk whose job it was to jostle the victim, possibly pushing him against a wall while the file picked his pocket

Filibuster – originally someone illegally fighting a war against another country (such as a mercenary, a buccaneer or a pirate) but came to mean acting in a way to obstruct a legislative assembly as, for example, by talking endlessly; the word filibuster originated in the late 18th century from the French word flibustier, which was applied to Pirates pillaging and so on in the Spanish colonies in the West Indies, it then came to mean American adventurers inciting revolution in Latin America

Fills a gentleman's eye – curvaceous woman, shapely and attractive (Victorians, who were nothing if not sexist, also said that if a woman were to fill a gentleman's eye she needed to 'possess thoroughly good points')

Find cold weather – to be thrown out of a lovely warm pub on a chilly night

Fine words butter no parsnips – empty words or flattery are of no value (first used in 1639)

Fine writing ink – sellers of ink worked the streets of London from at least the year 1600; the ink sellers cried out 'Fine writing ink' to attract customers and carried a barrel full of ink, a pint measure and a funnel; customers would buy a pint of ink and have it poured into their own container

Finger and thumb – rum (rhyming slang)

Fire box – man of all consuming passion ('My George is a real fire box,' she said.)

Fire priggers – men or women who pretend to help when there is a fire but who steal whatever they pretend to 'rescue' from the flames

Fireship – wench who has venereal disease and who is, therefore, a danger to all who sail near her

Firkin – small cask for butter, fish or other comestibles; also a measure of liquid volume equal to nine imperial gallons; firkin is a word which has come to us from Middle English and although a noun it is sometimes used as though it were a verb as in 'Stop firkin about Johnson!'

Fish-bagger – someone who lives in the suburbs, works in the city and does all their shopping in the city (spending little or nothing in the shops where they live); fish-baggers were as unpopular in olden times as second home owners are today in Devon, Cornwall and other holiday resorts

Fishy about the gills – drunk or recently drunk and still suffering

Fit in the arm – a blow (In 1897 a man called Tom Kelly was charged with hitting a woman. His defence was that he'd had a 'fit in his arm' which was what had caused the blow.)

Five o'clock tea – miserly tea consisting of a cup of tea and a thin slice of bread and butter and very little else

Fiveoclocquer – afternoon tea as described by Anglophones in Paris or Francophiles in London

Fizzle – a small, almost noiseless fart which may or may not have odiferous qualities

Flag of distress – bit of white shirt showing through a tear in a pair of trousers

Flagitious – villainous or criminal

Flague – to put ginger up a horse's fundament in order to ensure that he is lively and carries his tail well. A horse dealer's servant who showed a horse without doing this would be punished. The word is also used for showing encouragement.

Flam – white lie

Flaneur – someone who strolls (usually in a city) simply for the joy of seeing and being seen

Flapdoodle – nonsense, poppycock, balderdash; a wonderful word which first appeared in the mid 19th century (though no one knows where it came from) and which definitely deserves to be revived

Flapper – young girl, in her teens, unimpeded by morals (by the 1920s a flapper had become an older girl, keen on having a good time but still not too worried about social or moral constraints)

Flash – high class hooker ('the hotel was full of 'flash')

Flash o'light – woman dressed in very bright clothes

Flat as a frying pan – very flat

Fleece – 1) overcharge or swindle gullible or ignorant individuals such as tourists 2) woolly covering of a sheep or goat

Fleet – someone more enthusiastic about idling and messing about than they are about working (many modern employers complain that too many of their employees can be described as 'fleet')

Fleshy part of the thigh – a euphemism for the bum (the phrase was introduced when Lord Methuen was wounded in that part of his body while in South Africa)

Flibbertigibbet – flighty, frivolous and talkative (one of the most beautiful of the forgotten words – laws should be passed to ensure that this word regains its popularity)

Flight o'steps – thick slices of bread and butter

Flimflam – confidence trickery; a flim flam artist is a confidence trickster; the phrase may sound modern but it originated in the mid 16th century

Flimsy – thin, unsubstantial anything (paper, excuse or, today, an item of clothing sold online)

Fling – cheat

Flip – small beer, brandy and sugar; when lemon was also added the drink was called a Sir Cloudfly Shovel because a man of that name used to drink a good deal of it. Why is it that people no longer have wonderful names like 'Sir Cloudly Shovel'? I suspect that Charles Dickens took the wonderful names in his books from his neighbours rather than his imagination.

Flip-flap – fringe of hair across the forehead of a boy or youth

Floccinaucinihilipilification – estimating as worthless (long my favourite word, at school I endeavoured to squeeze it into every essay I wrote)

Florence – wench who has been towzed and ruffled (arrested for a breach of the peace and handcuffed)

Flounce – thick black paint on the lower eyelid to enhance the appearance of the eye

Flouting – ignore or disregard a law, rule or usual standard of behaviour

Flummery – insincere flattery and compliments as provided by public relations executives and sales persons but the word also describes a mixture of oatmeal and water

Flush in the pocket – to have loads of money

Fly loo – a gambling game played during summer. Players sit or stand around a table. Each player has a lump of sugar or a spoonful of honey in front of them. The winner is the one whose sugar or honey is first to attract a fly. This was not widely regarded as a game of skill. If a television company revived this game it would doubtless become a great success

Fly slicers – life guard soldiers sitting on horseback who can be seen driving away annoying flies with their swords

Flyer – to have sex without getting undressed or getting into bed

Flying camps – beggars working a funeral in the hope of being given money or food

Foal and filly dance – dance for children and young people

Fob – cheat or trick

Fogey – invalided soldier, usually has the word 'old' attached to it

Folderol – nonsense

Foot and mouth disease – swearing and kicking or, more accurately, kicking and swearing

Footman's mawnd – artificial sore on the back of the hand, made with rust, soap and lime and made to look as if resulting from a bite or the kick of a horse (the aim, of course, is to obtain money from the owner of the innocent horse)

Fopdoodle – simpleton, fool

Fopper – error (taken from the French words 'faux pas')

Foreigneering coves – foreigners (the Victorians and their forebears were not universally keen on foreigners)

Foreman of the jury – someone who dominates a conversation or speaks for the rest of the company

Forever-gentleman – once a gentleman always a gentleman; a well-bred fellow

Fork – pickpocket (according to an old book on 'how to pick pockets' it was claimed that the best way to take something from a pocket was to thrust the fingers straight into the pocket and to close them, hooking out what they had 'caught')

Forlorn hope – a gambler's last hope

Foundation garment – an item of clothing such as a corset, worn as underwear and designed to give the wearer a more acceptable figure; in the 17th, 18th and 19th centuries women used to wear vast amounts of underwear

Foundling – child abandoned in the streets and educated at the parish's expense

Fountain temples – public conveniences

Four legged fortune – a winning horse

Fourpenny cannon – beef steak pudding (sold for a groat)

Frample – peevish or sour; to be frampold is to be soured by life and experience

Franion – licentious person; but franions might also be idle wanderers so it is not beyond the bounds of possibility that a franion might be both an idle person and a licentious wanderer

Fraternity – gang, usually led by an 'upright' man (one of whose perks was to take first crack at all dells joining the gang – it wasn't only squires and gentry who enjoyed such perks)

Fraters – rogues, tricksters, but fraters were more specifically fraudulent collectors for charity who visited hospitals and other institutions

Freak – actors who lose their reputations by working in freak shows (which were looked down upon by most in the profession)

Freeholder – man whose wife accompanies him to the pub

French – used in the US to describe any unpopular fashion (Americans disliked foreigners even more than the English did)

French disease – venereal disease

French knickers – wide legged knickers, usually made of silk

French leave – to go off without saying goodbye (for example, to run away from creditors)

French worm – the pox; venereal disease

Frenchified – a man or woman who had venereal disease would say they were 'frenchified'

Frenchy – term of abuse aimed at any foreigner

Freshwater mariners – bogus old sailors whose tales owe more to imagination than to experience

Fribble – an effeminate fop

Friday face – dismal countenance seen at the end of the week since Friday was widely considered to be a day of abstinence from all good things

Fried carpets – very short ballet skirts (no one seems to know why a short tutu should have been described as a fried carpet, it is enough to know that they were)

Frisk – to dance the Paddington frisk was to be hanged

Frisky – bad tempered

Fritinancy – noises made by insects

Frivoller – someone with no serious aim in life

Front – audacity, cheek

Frowsty – warm and stuffy atmosphere (pub)

Fruit of a gibbet – corpse of a prisoner hanging on a gibbet

Frump – a high cut bodice, entirely covering the bosom and neck (in contrast to the low-cut bodices which were fashionable in the 1850s and 1860s, especially in Paris were female flesh was almost as visible as it is today at awards ceremonies)

Fubbs – fashionable curves, sensual chubbiness

Fubsey – plump wench

Fuddled – drunk

Fugleman – soldier who leads his fellows in a drill exercise; the word is derived in the early 19th century from the German word 'flugelmann' which means leader of the file; it isn't much of a stretch to suggest that the person running an exercise or aerobics class might be known as the fugleman, fuglewoman or, most probably, a fugleperson

Fulhams – loaded dice (either because they were made in Fulham or because there were a lot of sharpers in Fulham)

Full as a goat – drunk

Full-bosomed – woman considered to be well-endowed above the waist

Fun – to cheat or trick

Fungible – item replaceable by an identical item; the word arrived in the late 17th century from the Latin word 'fungibilis'

Fushionless – insipid, feeble

Fussock – fat and lazy woman

Fustian – pompous, pretentious and rather unbearably bombastic speech; almost all awards ceremony speeches are 'fustian', indeed this is particularly true of all school prize giving ceremony speeches; fustian is a Middle English word which, curiously, can also mean a thick, twilled cloth which has a short nap and is dyed

Fustilarian – menial person, scullery worker

Fusty lugs – well bosomed but beastly and slovenly woman

Futtock – middle timbers in a wooden ship's frame are known as futtocks; the word is Middle English

G

Gal-sneaker – scoundrel devoted to seduction

Galingale – gingery plant, used in herbal medicine and cookery; Middle English, derived either from Arabic or Chinese or French or, quite possibly, something else

Galliard – as a noun this means a man of spirit and fashion but as an adjective it means sturdy, brisk and lively (the word originally meant a lively dance with complicated steps but in the middle of the 16th century it began to take on its more modern meanings)

Galligaskins – very loose trousers, breeches; the word was originally used in the 16th century

Gallimaufry – a jumble or medley of things, first commonly used in the middle of the 16th century though the origin is mysterious; often used to describe a hotpot, stew or meal made up of leftovers

Gallipot – apothecary

Gally-pot baronet – doctor with an honour

Galoot – clumsy, stupid oaf; when the word was born in the early 19th century it meant an experienced sailor

Gambetter – a verb which means to humbug

Gambler – card sharp

Game – 'pigeons' drawn into a game or bawdy house to be cheated; alternative meanings include a young whore or someone being hung who dies without showing any signs of fear or repentance

Gander – fop

Gangrel – loafing lout

Ganymede – effeminate student

Gap stopper – whore master

Garbage – clothes

Garbed – fully dressed as opposed to, well, not fully dressed

Gardyloo – a warning shouted by house residents who lived in busy streets when they were about to empty a chamberpot from an upstairs window (the word is derived from the French gardez l'eau)

Garret election – a dotty ceremony practised at each new English parliament; two members were elected to represent the borough of Garrat (which was a few straggling cottages near Wandsworth in Surrey); the voters were those men who had enjoyed a woman in the open air within that district and the candidates were jesters who dressed themselves to look ridiculous; large numbers of people attend the election and the costs of the proceedings were met by local publicans

Garter – band of elastic or some other material used to hold up a stocking; the word is Middle English. (The oldest order of chivalry in England is the Most Noble Order of the Garter, which celebrated its 675th anniversary in 2023. It is said that the knighthood originated when Edward III was dancing with a lady whose garter fell to the ground. In a moment of rather bizarre gallantry, the king picked up the garter and put it on his own leg saying: 'Honi soit qui mal y pense' – which means, roughly, 'evil to him who evil thinks'. The phrase is now the motto of the Most Noble Order of the Garter.)

Gas-pipes – tight trousers

Gawkey – a thin, tall, awkward, young man or woman might be described as gawkey (or gawky)

Gay – as a noun, the word 'gay' traditionally referred to a prostitute (either male or female)

Gaze at the melody – look at something head on; face the music

Gentleman commoner – empty bottle (or a not well educated gentleman; a decent education was considered demeaning for a gentleman)

Gentleman of the back door – sodomite

Gentleman's master – highwayman

Gentry cove – gentleman

Gentry cove ken – gentleman's house

Gentry mort – gentlewoman

German duck – half a sheep's head, boiled with onions

Gerontocracy – government of a country or a society by old people

Get inside and pull the blinds down – a warning given when a poor rider approached since it was considered likely that one way or another he would want money

Get outside – swallow

Get up early – be bright, be clever

Get your eye in a sling – get a black eye

Getting a big boy now – getting a big boy now

Giblets – man and woman who cohabit without being married

Giddy young whelp – young man about town

Gigglemug – constantly smiling face

Gilflurt – proud, vain, capricious woman

Gilt – thief who picks locks; will sometimes open a public house, open doors and trunks and steal everything worth stealing from everyone; a gilt was also known as a rum dubber

Gin bottle – a dirty, abandoned, alcoholic woman

Gin crawl – now usually known as a pub crawl (once a common pastime among journalists, writers and unemployed actors though none of these would consider doing any such thing these days)

Gin palace – pub; the phrase was often used wittily about the scruffiest, most broken down of establishments

Gingangbobs – toys, bawbles, man's testicles

Gingerbread – cake made with treacle, flour and grated ginger; also refers to money

Girdle – strong material extending from the waist to the top of the thighs. A girdle may be rolled onto the body (hence the alternative, modern name of 'roll on') to give a smoother line

Git a bit – beggar's refrain

Git the ambulance – not feeling well, so please call the ambulance (or at least put me in the queue for one)

Git the sads – to have the vapours

Give it a lick and a promise – do something half-heartedly

Give it hot – a darned good telling off

Glabella – the area between nose and eyebrows is known as the glabella

Glazier – someone who breaks windows in order to steal what is inside or to be able to make money repairing them

Gleed – a glowing coal

Glib – smooth talking rogue

Glim – candle or lantern showing a modest light and therefore used in house breaking

Glimfenders – andirons

Glimmerers – confidence tricksters who falsely claim to have lost belongings or money in a fire

Glimstick – candlestick

Gluepot – parson (man who joins men and women together in marriage)

Gnatsnapper – rogue

Go between – pimp or bawd

Go on the aeger – join the sick list (used particularly by university students at Oxford)

Go on tick – borrow money

Go to bed – start the presses for printing a newspaper

Go without a passport – commit suicide

Goat – lascivious person

Godfathers – jury

Godfer – troublesome child

Goggles – large eyes

Going 'ome – dying

Going 'ter keep a peanner-shop – proposal of intended grandeur

Going to buy anything? – query put by a thirsty man to a newcomer entering a pub

Going to see a dog – going to see a woman

Gold dropper – trickster who drops a piece of gold (such as a ring) and then picks it up in full sight of the 'mark'; the 'mark' is then invited to a public house to have a celebratory drink but while there is robbed, often by being persuaded to take part in a rigged game of cards; sometimes the trickster finding the gold or ring will sell the item to the 'mark' at a ridiculously low price – only later will the 'mark' discover that the gold is brass not gold (See also 'drop a cog'; this trick is still tried on innocents and is, for example, extremely popular in Paris)

Gollumpus – large, clumsy fellow

Gongoozler – someone who stares idly and without purpose at something (anything) for a long time; a rather loveable word which just creeps into this book having originated in the early 20th century and, therefore, being one of the youngest words allowed entry; the word does, however, have a definite 19th century air to it

Gonoph – thief

Good egg – reliable, decent person

Good young man – hypocrite

Goose – a tailor's goose is a smoothing iron used to press down seams

Gooseberry-picker – go between helping to bring together a young couple

Goosecap – rogue

Gormacon – monster with six eyes, three mouths, four arms, eight legs (three on one side and five on the other), three arses and an arse upon its back (literally a man on horseback with a woman sitting side saddle behind him)

Gospel of the tub – unnatural enthusiasm for bathing in cold water

Got a clock – carrying a handbag

Got a collar on – snooty

Got the crop – military style haircut

Got the glow – to blush

Got the morbs – to feel sad

Got the pants – tired from over exertion

Got the shutters up – surly and uncommunicative (like a closed shop)

Got the woefuls – depressed, sad, miserable

Got up and dusted – escaped

Got up no end – very elegantly attired

Gotch gutted – pot bellied

Gotter dam-merung – expletive popular after the first performance of Wagner's The Ring in London in 1862

Gracile – slender and graceful

Gramercy – posh way of saying 'thank you very much'; derived from the French phrase 'grand merci' which means 'big thanks'; first used in the 14th century and so deserves the respect afforded the long-lived

Gray mare the better horse – the wife is a better person than the husband

Gray-mite – vegetarian

Grease – bribe

Greedy scene – scene in the theatre when a principal actor clears the stage to have all the attention

Green bag – attorney (lawyers often carried deeds in a green bag; unsuccessful lawyers filled their green bags with an old pair of breeches to make themselves look busy and successful

Greenhorn – novice; un-debauched young man

Gride – to scratch on something, as with nails on a blackboard; to make a grating sound; gride can also be a noun ('the gride he made set their teeth on edge')

Griminess – in literature this means eroticism; applied particularly to French fiction which was generally considered to be universally obscene though naturally it wasn't

Grin in a glass case – to be preserved as a skeleton in a glass case (many criminals were immortalised in this way)

Gripple – mean or stingy

Groak – to stare at people who are eating in the desperate hope that you will be given some food; all dogs are groaks

Grogging – adulterating alcohol by adding water

Gropers – blind men; midwives

Grouthead – blockhead, a stupid person

Grub Street – a street near Moorfields in London which was formerly the home of writers who worked for booksellers and so a Grub Street writer was a hack author

Grub Street news – lies and false information

Grumbletonian – discontented person

Gruntle – continuous lamentation

Guanoing the mind – reading French novels (the phrase was invented by Benjamin Disraeli, the English novelist and Prime Minister whose own novels were pretty unreadable)

Gudgeon – freshwater fish; easily fooled person; socket on a boat into which the rudder fits; pin holding two blocks of stone (or almost anything else) together; part of a hinge; bit of metal that keeps a gate closed; in short, a gudgeon is almost anything you want it to be

Guffoon – shambling, physically awkward individual

Gugusse – effeminate youth often found in the company of priests (the word was taken from a French novel about the priesthood)

Gulled – cheated, deceived

Gullgropers – usurers who lend money to gamesters

Gulosity – gluttony, greed

Gummed – no teeth left and therefore on his last legs

Gummy – has nothing to do with teeth, or a lack of them, but is taken from gommeux, a French word meaning generous, wise, tolerant and lots of other good things.

Gunner's daughter – to kill the gunner's daughter was to tie someone to a gun and flog them – on their bottoms

Gunpowder – old woman

Gutter Lane – the throat

Gutting a quart pot – emptying a pot; gutting and eating an oyster; cleaning a house of its contents

Guts and Garbage – very fat man or woman; more guts than brains

Guttle – eat greedily; the guttler eats just about anything as opposed to the gourmand who is a connoisseur of good food (but still probably eats too much) and the gourmet who has a discerning palate and is more continent

Guy – a dummy to be burnt; named after Guy Fawkes who took part in a plot to blow up the Houses of Parliament in November 1605 (the failure of the plot is still celebrated, though if the celebrants were wise they would mourn the failure)

Gyp – errand boy or scout at college in Oxford

Gypsies – vagrants who were feared because they were reputed to steal (often from farms)

H

Ha-Ha – ditch built as a boundary in a park or large garden; (without the hyphen the phrase simply means 'very funny'); the ha-ha originated in the 18th century and was built to enable country home owners to enjoy their view of their animals without worrying about the animals getting too close to the house; wildlife parks use ha-has instead of fences to control wild animals and it is possible to stand and watch a rhinoceros charging towards you safe in the knowledge that the creature will halt when it reaches the ha-ha and won't suddenly decide that it can leap the ditch or just go through it

Haberdasher – draper, dealer in laces and ribbons

Haberdasher of pronouns – schoolmaster

Haggis debate – discussions about Scotland

Hairpin – simpleminded person

Hake – someone from St Ives in Cornwall (referring to the likelihood of his smelling of fish)

Half a ton of bones done up in horsehair – ropey looking horse that isn't much good for anything

Half-hour gentleman – fellow with superficial breeding

Half-past nines – large boots or shoes for a woman

Half up the pole – nearly drunk

Hamlets – silly word for omelettes, started by actors appearing in Hamlet in London

Hammered – married

Hang an arse – to hang back, to be afraid to go forward

Hang up – shut up

Hang up the ladle – get married

Hangman's Wages – thirteen pence and a halfpenny was the fee (this included a shilling for performing the execution and three half pence for providing the rope) – this at least was the fee paid in the 18th century

Hanky panky – slightly dubious or improper behaviour; with some suggestion of sexual impropriety (this phrase was first used in the 1840s and it has to be admitted that what was then dismissed as of little consequence would today probably be considered serious enough to merit the attention of the police, a human resources department the entire social media community and, inevitably, those mainstream media commentators who take a dim view of such things

Happy tablet home – a nursing home, often specialising in the care of the elderly or the mentally ill

Haptephobia – fear of being touched

Hardware – ammunition

Harridan – bossy woman; worn out harlot

Harum Scarum – used to describe anyone running or walking in a hurry – and doing so carelessly

Have a turn – fight

He worships his creator – self-made man who thinks he did a darned fine job

Heap of coke – bloke

Heap o' saucepan lids – money (rhyming slangs because it rhymes with dibs; this must be one of the more obscure examples of rhyming slangs and it was only really popular with members of the hardware trade and their customers)

Heathen philosopher – a man whose clothes are falling apart, with underclothing visible through the holes

Heaver – breast

Heavy baggage – wives and children

Heavy-breasted – exactly what it suggests

Heavy hand – lot of trouble

Hebetude – dullness or stupidity; early 17th century;

Heckling – modest bullying, if bullying can ever be modest

He-male – male (as opposed to she-male which was a female but is not necessarily so these days)

Hedge – to cover a bet by taking odds on both sides so that whatever happens there is a profit

Hedge whore – itinerant harlot who disposes of her favours independently (often under a hedge) and without the help of a bawdy house proprietor

Hedge alehouse – small obscure inn

Heliotrope – a purple colour, most commonly appearing in the manufacture of pyjamas and underclothing

Hell – place where stolen goods (called cabbage) are kept

Hell born babe – lewd, graceless youth of a wicked disposition

Hell cat – furious, scolding woman; a vixen

Hempen fever – a man who was hung was said to have died of 'hempen fever' (in Dorset he was said to have been stabbed with a Bridport dagger since ropes used for hanging were made there)

Hen hearted – cowardly

Hen house – home where the woman rules

Henchman –trusted companion, supporter and follower; from the Old English; originally complimentary but now probably used more pejoratively

Heye-glass weather – foggy or misty weather

Hidgeot – idiot in street parlance

High collar and short shirts – someone pretending to be posher than they truly are

High jinks – dice gambler who drinks to get his pigeon or mark intoxicated

High water – flush with money

Highfalutin – pompous or pretentious language; from the 19th century

Hill-top literature – good advice (derived from the signs at the top of steep hills warning cyclists of the danger that lies ahead)

Hinchinarfer – woman with a deep voice but the capacity to shriek on occasion

Hippocampelephantocamelos – red nose (they should rename 'red nose day' and then insist that everyone involved says the new name)

Hirple – to limp; to proceed with a slow and painful motion

Hither and yon (also hither and thither) – travel in various directions

Ho! he's got the white coat – he is drunk

Hoast – wheezy cough

Hob or nob – One explanation is that drinkers would ask one another 'Will you hob or nob with me?' (will you drink a glass of wine with me); if the reply was 'nob' then the challenged man could choose whether to drink red or white wine. An alternative explanation, and to my mind better explanation, comes from the fact that in the days of Queen Elizabeth I big chimneys and huge hearths were in fashion. At the corner of each hearth there was a small elevated projection called the hob. Behind the hob there was a seat. In winter time, beer was placed upon the hob to warm up. The cold beer was placed on a small table in the room. The small table was called a job. And so 'Will you hob or no?' meant, would you like warm beer from the hob or cold beer from the nob?

Hobbled – impeded

Hobbledehoy – a clumsy youth

Hobby horse – a man's favourite amusement; also a small toy horse given to children

Hobnail – country clodhopper (from shoes being full of hob nails and tipped with iron to prevent them wearing out)

Hobson's choice – a carrier in Oxford used to rent horses to students but never let them choose their mount, always selecting the horse for the student. The carrier's name was Hobson

Hocus – drunk

Hocus pocus – originally the conjuror, now the two words refer just to the words uttered to accompany the conjuror's trick

Hoddy doddy – all arse and no body; a short clumsy person

Hoisting – ceremony for new soldiers who have been recently married. Three or four men in the same company as the new groom would seize him, putting two bayonets into his hat (to represent horns) and then hoist him onto their shoulders. The new groom would be carried round with music from a drum and fife accompanying his journey. This parade was known as the 'cuckold's march'

Holborn Hill – criminals being taken to Tyburn for execution went up Holborn Hill and travelled backwards so that they didn't have to look at the gallows awaiting them. The last public execution at Tyburn took place in 1784. After that criminals were executed near Newgate.

Holding up the corner – loafer standing on a street corner, and possibly holding up the joined building (cf Harpo Marx)

Home rulers – potatoes baked on a street stall

Homunculus – very small but normally formed person; originated in the middle of the 17th century

Honey moon – the first month after a marriage

Hooker – prostitute (hookers are named after an American Civil War general of that name who provided prostitutes for his soldiers and who was repaid his kindness by having his family name commemorated forever in this way)

Hookers and anglers – people who carry a staff with a crook, to lift things to steal them

Hooray Henry – lively but ineffectual man with no discernible skills or qualities; an upper class twit

Hop the twig – to run away

Hop merchant – dancing master, also known as a caper merchant

Hopper arsed – someone with large, projecting buttocks

Horbgorble – to putter about in an ineffective way

Hornified – cuckolded

Hornswoggle – to cheat

Horse godmother – large, masculine looking woman

Hot green peas – from the year 1400 until Victorian times the cry of 'hot green peas' could be heard on London's streets; sellers carried peas, cooked in their shells, on a tin pan, with a cloth over them to keep them warm, and offered customers butter, salt and pepper

Hot potato – waiter (more Cockney rhyming slang)

House – group of people who always sit together at parties

House-proud – worker who lives in their own cottage (a surprising number of workers owned the property they lived in during the 19th century)

Housebreaker – demolition worker (a rare, literal definition)

Howells-and-scrape – vulgar and rather purposeless cheap fiction (derived from the names of two American authors called Howells and Scrape)

Howler – fop or swell

Howling comique – terrible comic singer

Hoyden – boisterous girl, described in the 18th century as a 'romping girl'

Hubris – insolence (a word which has slowly gravitated towards arrogance)

Huckster – itinerant retailer of provisions

Huffle – 16th century word which, according to Captain Grose (writing in his dictionary published in 1811) describes 'a piece of bestiality too filthy for explanation'

Huffy – to take offence at small things

Hug centre – a park where a good deal of love-making goes on

Hugger-mugger – means stealthily and privately but also may mean frivolously; the word first appeared early in the 16th century

Hullo, features – greeting on meeting a chum

Hum – to hum or to humbug is to deceive

Hum box – pulpit in a church

Hum drum – tedious teller of tales; a bore

Hump – once a fashionable term for copulation (probably originating in the early 18th century)

Humpty dumpty – small rather clumsy person of either sex

Hums – member of the congregation at a church service

Hunder hand – sudden blow, given without warning

Hunks – jealous, miserly fellow

Hunting the squirrel – game enjoyed by post boys and coachmen who would follow a one horse chaise to harass it, and then pass it very close by with the intention of terrifying the occupant (usually a woman)

Hurdy gourdy (hurdy gurdy) – kind of fiddle made out of a gourd

Hurly burly – riot or confusion in the street

Hussy – originally an abbreviation of housewife but by the 18th century it was used as a term of reproach

Hypergelast – someone who laughs excessively (in the 1970s they would be invited to TV comedy programme recordings but these days they probably just annoy fellow travellers by laughing at nonsense on their iPhone)

I

Ichabod – a lamentation (from the Bible)

Impostume – boil

Impressionist – something appealing directly to the emotions

In Paris – eloped (young couples can elope anywhere, of course, but it always used to be assumed that they had gone to Paris – which sounds romantic and distant enough – and I do remember once seeing a runaway couple sitting in a café in St Germain, apparently either blissfully unaware that their pictures were on the front pages of all the English newspapers on sale at a kiosk just twenty feet away or unconcerned about it; he was a school teacher and she was a pupil and neither seemed under duress and so naturally I did not dob them in)

In the drag – behind

Incident – an unexpected pregnancy and/or an illegitimate child

Incunabula – books in existence that were printed before 1500 (that's the year 1500, not 3 o'clock in the afternoon by continental time); despite rumours none of my books was written or published before 1500

Ineffable – too extreme to be described in words (other than this one); from the Middle English

Ingravescent – a medical condition which is gradually deteriorating; early 19th century, derived from the same word in Latin which means 'growing heavy' or 'getting worse'

Inkle weavers – brotherly people

Inkslinger – clerk (one of my favourite words and one which I would love to see brought back into common use)

Imposthume – a boil

Inchoate – beginning or just begun

Ineluctable – inescapable, irresistible

Innocents – weak or simple people

Inspissate – thicken or congeal; from Latin word 'inspissat ('made thick') and in English from the early 17th century

Introduce shoemaker to tailor – metaphor for to kick someone's bum (the Victorians preferred to deal with minor problems themselves, rather than making complaints, running to the local police station or rushing to update their Facebook pages, and kicking a miscreant in the fundament was apparently a common remedy for misbehaviour)

Irish apricots – potatoes

Irish draperies – cobwebs

Irish evidence – false witness

Irish toothache – pregnancy

Iron – money

Italian quarrel – remorseless treachery

Ithyphallic – statue or painting of a deity with an erect penis; or a sexually explicit poem; early 17th century from the Greek word 'ithuphallikos' which means straight phallus

Ivy bush – weazle faced man with bushy hair or a large wig

J

Jabber – to talk quickly, to chatter like a magpie or a preacher; also used to describe someone speaking in a foreign language as in 'he jabbered to me in French or some other foreign language, but naturally I could not understand him'

Jack – a rather knavish fellow, hence the 'knave' in a pack of cards is known as the Jack (first appeared in the middle of the 16th century)

Jack of legs – tall, long legged man or giant; the original 'Jack of legs' was a robber who lived in a wood and who was renowned for plundering the rich to feed the poor; when he was captured and sentenced to death he asked to have his bow and arrow put into his hand and to be allowed to shoot an arrow, being buried where the arrow fell; the arrow fell in a churchyard where he was duly buried. (I have no evidence for this but it does seem possible that Little John, of Robin Hood fame, could be based on the same individual.)

Jack Robinson – to say 'before I could say Jack Robinson' is a saying which means in a very short time; the original Jack Robinson was described a volatile fellow who would call on his neighbours but be gone before his name could be announced ('He was gone before I could say Jack Robinson'.)

Jack Sprat – dwarf

Jack Weight – fat man

Jackanapes – cheeky or impertinent person; originally, in the 16th century used to describe a monkey called Jack Napes

Jacked it – died

Jacket – to threaten to jacket someone is to threaten to have them locked up in an asylum or loony bin where they will be placed in a straight jacket

Jacktation – boasting

Jam – pretty girl. Notorious girls of easy virtue, working in Piccadilly, London were originally known as tarts and then they called themselves jam tarts (asking potential clients if they would like a jam tart) and then they became known simply as jam.

Jammiest bits of jam – beautiful, young girls, perfect in every way

Jape – practical joke or prank, sometimes quite complicated, of the kind perpetrated by schoolboys, usually at boarding schools such as Frank Richards' Greyfriars where Billy Bunter was a pupil

Jarkman – sham clergy who specialise in false marriages; the word is also used to describe the forgers who fabricate counterfeit passes and licences for beggars

Jaw – speech, conversation

Jejune – simplistic, naïve, uninteresting

Jeremiad – a list of woes

Jeremiah mongering – doomsters who always see the worst happening

Jerking a wheeze – a wheeze is a gag or joke and jerking a wheeze is telling a joke well

Jerry sneak – henpecked husband; a man governed by his wife

Jerrycummumble – shake or tumble about

Jew – hard, sharp fellow; any extortioner

Jew bail – not enough money for bail money

Jezebel – immoral, shameless woman (who would probably have had an Instagram account and major presence on TikTok if those had been available in the 19th century)

Jib – flat folding chimney pot hat

Jig – trick

Jilt – crafty woman who encourages the advances of a man whom she intends to deceive

Jilted – man rejected by a woman

Jimmy Fellow – smart fellow

Jimmy Rounds – Frenchmen (this comes from the French 'je me rends' which was rumoured to be the cry uttered by all Frenchmen when confronted with an English sailor)

Jinks the Barber – spy or informant (from the fact that barbers do tend to like to share gossip with their customers)

Job – hen pecked husband

Jobberknoll – a small bird which makes no sound until it is about to die; also the human head when spelt Jobbernole

Jocund – light-hearted, cheerful, jolly

Jock – to enjoy the attentions of a woman ('he spent the evening jocking')

Jockum gage – chamber pot

John Fortnight – tallyman who calls every other week to collect money

Johnny Bum – a jackass (the word was used by ladies trying to show that they were too refined to use the word 'jack' because it was vulgar word and would not use the word 'ass' because that too was considered improper)

Joined the angels – died

Joint – wife

Jolly – head

Jolly dog – merry fellow, bon vivant happy to have a good time

Jolly Roger – flag favoured by pirates, also known as the skull and crossbones because it showed the skull and crossbones

Jolthead – foolish or stupid individual

Jordan – chamber pot

Jorum – large bowl used for serving drinks

Josser – a grand person or grandee; something of a swell

Jounce – to jolt or bounce

Jove – another name for Jupiter; the exclamation 'By Jove' dates from the 16th century

Judy slayer – lady killer

Juggins's Boy – impudent son of a dim-witted father

Juggins-hunting – to look for someone prepared to pay for alcohol

Jumblegut lane – rough road or lane which throws travellers all over the place; a potholed thoroughfare

Jumbo – anything large, outsized

Jumped up swell – someone who has gone from rags to riches

Junoesque – tall and shapely woman

Jury leg – wooden leg

K

Kakistocracy – government by the worst citizens (many would argue that we've all been living in kakistocracies for decades if not for centuries)

Kangaroo – thin, tall man

Kansas neck-blister – big knife, specifically a Bowie knife

Kate – lock picker or picklock

Katterzem – man willing to go out to dinner for a free meal (often to make up a table where there would otherwise be 13 guests); the word was also used to describe a parasite

Kedogenous – a condition brought about by worry or anxiety; any stress related disorder

Keep off the grass – be careful, watch out

Keep the devil out of one's clothes – battle against poverty

Keep up old queen – one woman cheering another who is being taken to prison

Keep your 'air on – recommending patience

Keeping cully – a man who keeps a mistress for his own use may well be keeping her for public use (that's 'keeping cully')

Keeping Dovercourt – making a lot of noise

Kemp's shoes – lucky omen; throwing shoes was considered lucky and throwing Kemp's shoes was considered particularly fortuitous, though presumably not for Kemp (the phrase originated with a play by Ben Johnson)

Ken – house

Ken cracker – housebreaker

Ken miller – housebreaker

Kent Street Ejectment – to remove the street door, so leaving the house open; this practice was popular with landlords in parts of London when tenants were more than two weeks in arrears with their rent

Kerwollop – to beat or wallop someone

Ketch – popular name for hangmen; originated with Jack Ketch who was hangman in 1682 and some years after; Mrs Ketch said that any bungler could hang a man but only her husband knew how to make a gentleman die sweetly

Kettle drums – breasts

Khaki – colour once called Devonshire grey (chosen to replace the scarlet uniform previously worn by British army, the army authorities having realised at last that the scarlet colour made soldiers a clear target for the enemy)

Kick – look for work

Kicks – breeches

Kid lay – rogue who defrauds errand boys or young apprentices, carrying goods in their charge e.g. by offering to take care of a parcel or to help deliver it

Kidney – disposition, humour as in 'he was of a strange kidney'

Kill with kindness – not quite what it seems; actually means offering false sympathy to someone who has misbehaved

Killing the canary – avoiding work

Kinchin – small child, often an orphan beggar boy as recruited by Fagin in Dicken's novel 'Oliver Twist'

Kinching coes – male child beggar and general delinquent

Kinching morts – female child beggar and general delinquent

King's pictures – money

Kiss-curl – flat curl on the forehead

Kissing crust – first cut from a loaf

Kit – dancing master; so called because dancing masters carried with them a small fiddle called a kit

Kitchen physic – good food

Kitling – a very young kitten

Kittle – tickle

Kittle pitchering – a fun way of hobbling or silencing a boring person telling a long boring story; this is done by contradicting some irrelevant part of the story and allowing or encouraging others to join in the side issue with the result that the main story (the long, boring story) is forgotten about

Klobber – best clothes

Knack shop – toy shop, also known as a nicknackatory

Knave – dishonest and unscrupulous male

Knee-drill – hypocritical prayer

Knickerbockers – breeches which are gathered at calf or knee and rather loose fitting (plus fours and plus sixes, as once favoured by golfers, are a type of knickerbocker)

Knickers – late 19th century word used in Britain; item of women's underclothing covering the body from the waist to the tops of the legs and containing two holes for the legs

Knife – shrewish woman

Knight and barrow pig – someone who pretends to be a gentleman but who is more of a hog; a pretender who assumes a status not his own

Knight of the blade – bully

Knight of the post – someone prepared to swear to anything if paid to do so

Knight of the rainbow – footman, so-called because footmen were offered attired in colourful liveries

Knight of the road – highwayman

Knight of the shears – tailor

Knight of the thimble – tailor or stay maker

Knights of the jemmy – burglar

Knock – to have carnal knowledge

Knocker on the front door – to have a knocker on your front door was a real sign of respectability and of 'having arrived'

Knot – crew

Knows how many go to a dozen – sharp and alert

Knuckle confounders – ruffles which get in the way of pickpockets

Knuckles – thuggish pickpockets

Kyacting – fooling around while supposed to be working

L

La-di-da – posh, with money to spend and no work to do

Laced mutton – woman

Lacing – beating; as in 'one more word out of you and I'll lace your jacket handsomely'

Lady – hump backed woman

Lady bird – lewd woman

Lady Jane – plump, handsome woman with a merry disposition

Lady of easy virtue – prostitute

Lally-gagging – flirting

Lambskin men – judges

Lancinating – a sharp pain, described as cutting or tearing

Land o' Cakes – Scotland

Land loper – thief who hangs around in the countryside, pilfering small items (also known as a land lubber)

Land pirate – highwayman

Langtries – wonderful eyes (as a result of Mrs Lily Langtree whose portraits were everywhere, in both England and America, and who was famous for her beauty – her Christian name was also spelt Lillie)

Language of flowers – traditional guide to the meaning behind individual flowers (roses are for love and so on – my first published book was a version of The Language of Flowers) but also refers to the fact that a magistrate at Bow Street Police Court in London between 1860 and 1883 was a Mr Flowers whose favourite sentence was 'Ten shillings or seven days'. This was known as the 'language of Flowers'

Lansprisado – a lancer who is reduced to working because of the death of his horse

Lanthorn jawed – thin faced person; also someone who is an agent taking a bribe on behalf of his master

Lapidary – cutting, polishing and engraving stones and gems; a Middle English word

Larrikin – maverick, boisterous, badly behaved

Larking – described by Captain Grose, in his dictionary, as 'a lascivious practice that will not bear explanation' and so, taking the good Captain's advice I shall leave it at that

Larry Dugan's Eye Water – blacking for shoes, named after Larry Dugan who was a famous shoe black in Dublin

Last shake of the bag – youngest child

Latch-key – crowbar (burglars and bailiffs used crowbars instead of keys)

Lathy – thin person, almost as slender as a lath

Latitat – lawyer

Law – to give law to a hare was to give it a chance; the phrase 'to give law' was also used about giving someone a chance to escape or profit

Laystall – dunghill wherein 'soil' (sewage) from houses is dumped

Lazar of Venice – the pox; venereal disease

Lazybones – an instrument, a pick up stick with tongues, designed to enable fat, disabled or old people to pick up things which have fallen to the ground (still made and used in the same way)

Leaderette – short, pitchy 'leader' articles in newspapers

Leading article – best buy in a shop; priced to bring in customers in the hope that they will buy something else

Leading heavies – stage roles for middle aged actresses

Leaky – someone who cannot be trusted not to blab

Learning shover – schoolmaster

Leather – to leather someone is to beat them

Leather and prunella – something flimsily made (corruption of lather and prunella, with the lather being whipped cream and the prunella being damson or plum jam or jelly)

Leave him to fry in his own fat – give him enough rope and he'll hang himself

Leesome – lovable

Leptosome – having pleasingly slender body

Let her rip – go full out (taken from the habit of Mississippi steam boat captains forcing their boats to travel as fast as possible – with the result that the boiler would burst or rip)

Letter-fencers – postmen

Liberty bodice – invented at the end of the 19th century as part of the emancipation of women; a sleeveless, cotton, waist length covering which might be fleece lined. It usually buttoned up the front and had either buttons or suspenders to fasten on to knickers

Lickspittle – parasite or tale teller or snitch

Light food – chewing tobacco

Like to meet her in the dark – a plain woman

Limb of the law – pettifogging attorney

Line of the old author – dram of brandy

Lingerie – technically, any underwear or nightwear designed for women; the word is 19th century French and originally meant any feminine undergarments. Today it usually refers to lighter, flimsier undergarments, particularly those which are appealing to the eye or which have an erotic flavour

Lingo language – French or some other foreign tongue
Listening to oneself – thinking
Little bag of sugar – nice surprise
Little deers – young women keen to go onto the stage
Loap – run away
Lobby through – get a piece of legislation accepted through lobbying influence
Lobcock –stupid blunderer; someone not very bright who makes many mistakes; also a large, limp penis
Loblolley boy – surgeon's assistant on a ship
Locksmith's daughter – a key ('I've lost the locksmith's daughter')
Loge – a watch
Loggerhead – blockhead or stupid person
Loll – favourite child, mother's darling
London smoke – yellowish grey colour ('London smoke' was a popular colour for painting houses because it hid the dirt)
Long meg – tall woman
Long shanks – long legged
Long stomach – big appetite
Loo – the community; to say 'for the good of the loo' meant 'for the good of the community'
Loobies – ignorant, rather pathetic men
Look through your fingers – pretend something is not happening; to pretend not to see
Looking as if he hadn't got the right change – angry and wild
Looking glass – chamber pot, also known as a member mug
Looking like a widow woman – looking old
Looking seven ways for Sunday – squinting
Loony bin – a residential home for the mentally ill
Loose bit of goods – young woman who has abandoned the straight and narrow path of righteousness

Lorgnette – pair of glasses held in front of the eyes with the aid of a long handle fixed to one side (early 19th century, from the French word 'lorgner' which means 'to squint')

Lost a cartful and found a waggon-load – putting on weight

Lotties and Totties – women, particularly skimpily dressed girls seen in the stalls at music hall theatres or at night clubs

Loubard or lubbard – hooligan

Lounge – place for gossiping

Lousetrap – comb

Lout – uncouth man or youth (from 16th century)

Love curls – curls over the forehead

Lovely as she can be and live – a real beauty (if she were any more beautiful she would be an angel)

Low tide – when a man has no money it is low tide

Lubber – awkward fellow

Lubricious – 1) deliberately displaying secondary sexual characteristics 2) slippery

Lucifugous – shunning the light (a mid-17th century word)

Lugs – ears or wattles

Lungis – a tall and clumsy man

Lush – strong beer

Lusk – sloth

Lustrate – purify by ceremonial washing, sacrifice or some other ritual

Lye – urine

M

Mace – a mace is a rogue who pretends to be a gentleman so that he can defraud workmen or take advantage of people by borrowing money or a watch

Mackintosh – raincoat; named after a Scotsman called Charles Mackintosh who invented a lightweight fabric which was waterproof

Mad, Bad and Dangerous to Know – phrase used by Lady Caroline Lamb about her lover Lord Byron; the phrase has been used many times since, most notably by Ranulph Fiennes for his autobiography

Mad Tom – an abram; rogue who pretends to be mad

Madam – kept woman

Made – stolen

Made in Germany – badly made and of little value (please don't arrest me, I'm just reporting this stuff)

Madge – the private parts of a woman are her 'madge'

Madge culls – sodomites, homosexuals

Magniloquent – high flown, bombastic style of speaking

Magnoperate – to exalt, behave earnestly; usually to exaggerate someone's greatness

Magotty – whimsical

Maiden sessions – sessions where none of the prisoners are sentenced to be hung or otherwise executed

Malapropism – use of the wrong word, often with comic effect; derived from a comic character called Mrs Malaprop, who appeared in Richard Brinsley Sheridan's play 'The Rivals' and whose accidents with the English language have greatly amused audiences for generations

Malkintrash – someone dressed in dismal clothing

Malmsey nose – red, pimpled nose

Maltworm – drinker

Mammiform – breast; old English word from the Latin

Man of the town – rake, debauched man

Manque – failure to become something one wishes to be e.g. 'writer manque', 'politician manque' etc., etc.; dates back to late 18th century; the implication is that the individual concerned has dashed hopes and a life of some disappointment

Mantrap – defined as 'a woman's commodity'

Marchpane – marzipan (marchpane is simply the archaic spelling)

Margery – effeminate man

Marine officer – empty bottle

Marksman – legal term for a man who cannot write and simply makes his mark on documents (his mark usually being a cross)

Marm-puss – overdressed landlady

Marmalade – word possibly taken from melimelum, the honey apple. The earliest marmalade was made from quinces. (A 17th century traveller, journeying before British Rail snack-bars were opened, reported that he took macaroons, quince marmalade and wine as a snack when he left home.) Marmalade can be made from every fruit under the sun and cherry marmalade was once popular. There is a silly tale that when she felt queasy, Mary Queen of Scots would ask for a jam made of fruit. 'Marie malade', the court would say. Hence the word marmalade. This is probably nonsense but it is a pleasant etymological excursion.

Marmalade madam – a strumpet

Marmalet – another word for marmalade

Marriage music – squalling of children

Married – two people handcuffed or chained together while being taken to gaol

Married the widow – things going badly (the widow is the guillotine)

Mary Ann – effeminate man

Mashing – a dandy who behaves in a way which shows that he is rather pleased with himself

Master of the rolls – baker

Matrilocal – custom in which a husband lives with his wife and her relatives

Matrix – the environment in which something develops; the womb or a mould

Maudlin drunk – drunk in tears

Maulid – very drunk or soundly beaten

Mawnding – begging

Meacock – rogue

Mealy mouthed – over modest

Meater – coward

Medium body, elegant, very ready – not a woman or a motor car but a claret

Meed – an individual's deserved share of the praise or approbation

Megrim – headache, migraine

Mellow – jolly but not quite drunk

Melt – knock money off a bill; also to spend money

Member music – chamber pot

Mended – bandaged

Merkin – pubic hair wig for women (I first discovered this word when I was a medical student and managed to surprise professors and lecturers by working it into a surprising number of essays and conversations); the word 'merkin' first appeared in the early 17th century and I have still to discover why a woman would want a merkin and how she would fix it into place; I am also at a loss to explain why there was no equivalent demand among men for merkins

Merry begotten – bastard

Metempsychosis – the transmigration at death of a human soul into a new body of the same or a different species (from the 16th century)

Metile – semen (and so 'to fetch mettle'…)

Mettlesome – bold

Miasma – unpleasant, oppressive, unhealthy smell

Midge – sneak

Miffy – a fit of peevish ill humour but originally used to mean shabby

Mignon – dainty

Milch cow – someone easily tricked out of their money and/or property

Milk-bottle – baby

Milk the pigeon – try the impossible

Milksop – indecisive and/or cowardly man or boy

Mill – rob

Miller – murderer

Million to a bit of dirt – good bet

Mine-jobber – cheat

Mine Uncle's – pawnbroker

Minkin – small person or small pin

Mint – gold

Mish Topper – coat

Misleading paper – The Times newspaper in late 19th century (any newspaper today)

Miss – harlot

Mitten – refusal of offer of marriage ('she gave him the mitten')

Mizzling – disappearing, sauntering, moving slowly

Mobocracy – government or rule by a mob; first used in 1754 (also known as pollarchy)

Moll – whore

Moll-hunters – men chasing women

Molly – effeminate man, sodomite

Monday mice – black eyes appearing on Monday, after drunken beatings at the weekend

Monkey – prance about, flirt, be effusive towards a pretty girl; also, strangely, to suck wine out of a cask with a straw

Monocle – single eye glass which is held in place by scrunching up the muscles around that eye; the monocle may be attached by a cord to the user's coat

Moonling – a dreamy fool

Moppet – similar to honey, peach, kitten or flower

Mops, brooms and brushes – from the 18th century onwards street traders sold mops and brooms, crying out suitable advertising slogans as they patrolled the streets; by the middle of the 20th century, salesmen were selling mops, brooms and brushes door to door; weary looking men would lug huge suitcases around, hoping to sell their wares to housewives (my mother, I remember, would always feel sorry for the brush salesman and would generally buy something, whether she needed it or not; even as a young boy I recognised that the success of the salesman probably depended to a considerable extent upon his talent for invoking a sympathetic response from the housewives he visited – he also relied upon the fact that most women were professional housewives and did not go out to work)

Mopsy – term of endearment first used in 16th century; used to address a girl or small woman

Mort – a girl who is neither married nor a virgin; though how this could be is, of course, a mystery

Mother – water (another daft bit of rhyming slang, this from 'mother and daughter')

Mount the cart – be hanged (person about to be hung would stand on a cart with a rope around his neck, the cart would be driven away, leaving the criminal hanging; this device was often used in movies about the Wild West)

Mountebank – someone who deliberately deceives others: traditionally a trader who sold worthless medicines to the public

Mousetrap – marriage (also known as the parson's mousetrap)

Mouth-pie – scolding from a woman

Moveables – jewellery or other small items of value

Mrs Philip's Ware – a condom (Mrs Philips was the top maker and seller of condoms in London in the 1700s; she sold her wares to 'France, Spain, Portugal, Italy and other foreign places' and advertised that 'Captains of ships and gentlemen going abroad, may be supplied with any quantity of the best goods on the shortest notice'; her condoms (known as 'instruments of safety') were made from skins or bladders and were widely considered to be a notable improvement on the traditional condoms which had been made of tortoiseshell

Muck and halfpenny afters – rotten dinner with a cheap pudding (probably consisting of stewed prunes with lumpy custard)

Muckender – handkerchief

Mud lark – hog

Mud show – agricultural show

Muff – a young man who is a sap or a boob or both and also lazy; but despite all this rather amiable; a muff is also the private parts of a woman

Muffin-wallopers – women who love to gossip and discuss scandal over a cup of tea and a biscuit

Muffishness – soft and effeminate

Muffling cheat – napkin

Muggle – an ignorant person

Mugwump – someone who backs down, withdraws

Muliebrity – essence of womanhood, womanliness; from the 16th century and derived from the Latin

Mulligrub – depression

Mumchance – silent or tongue tied and rather doleful

Mumpers – originally mumpers were genteel beggars but gradually the adjective genteel was dropped

Mundane – fashionable person, male or female

Mundungus – entails, tripe, waste animal matter unfit to eat; also means nasty, rancid, putrid smelling tobacco

Museum headache – pain in the head caused by museum attendants, etc.

Mush, gush and lush – reviews or criticism paid for in money or food

Music Hall howl – strange style of singing heard from music hall artists who were keen for the audience to hear the words (usually so that they could sing along with the chorus)

Mussitation – almost inaudible mutterings, grumblings and murmurings; silent movement of the lips

Mustard plaster – dismal young man

Mute – undertaker's servant

Mutton headed – stupid

Mutton shunter – policeman on the beat

My elm is grown – I can see my own death coming (elm was used for making coffins)

Myrmidon – follower or servant, possibly unscrupulous, originally those working for a constable

N

Nail a goss – steal a hat (hats were called 'goss' because they were as light as gossamer; most people wore one and they were expensive so they were worth stealing and there was a ready market for them)

Nail a strike – steal a watch

Namby-pamby – weak, ineffectual and fearful

Nana – outrageous, indecent (from the novel Nana by Emil Zola)

Nancy – slightly effeminate

Nancy tales – humbug

Nanny house – brothel

Napper – head

Napper of Naps – sheep stealer

Nap or nothing – all or nothing

Nark the titter – watch that woman

Nattermy – thin human being

Near and far – bar (rhyming slang)

Neck stamper – boy who collects pots lent out from a pub to people in private houses

Necromancer – someone who communicates (or claims to communicate) with the dead

Needful – money

Needle – irritated

Negligee – mid 18th century word from the French; a light, filmy dressing gown which shows nothing but nevertheless tends to reveal more than it hides (from the verb negliger – to neglect)

Negus – port wine and hot water with grated nutmeg sprinkled into the drink

Neopolitan bone ache – the pox; venereal disease

Nepotation – extravagance, squandering money on riotous living; (from time to time a modern film, music or sports star who has gone bankrupt will say, with something of a wry smile, 'I spent 90% of my money on wine and women and wasted the rest' – that's nepotation)

Nescience – ignorance; taken from Middle English; the Middle English folk took it from the Latin word nescient which means 'not knowing'

Nettled – peevish, in a bad mood; described as 'a man or woman who has pissed on a nettle'

Neurasthenia – once a common diagnosis though with a variety of very ill-defined; symptoms usually including tiredness, irritability and emotional lability (neurasthenia still exists, albeit under a variety of different names)

Never squedge – duffer who seems to be without a pulse

Nice place to live – awful place to live

Nick name – name given in contempt or ridicule, from the French nom de nique

Nicknackatory – toy shop

Nightman – man whose job it was to empty soil buckets; this was usually done at night and the operation was called a wedding

Nimiety – extravagance, excess

Niminy-piminy – prim, refined, ladylike, effeminate; from the late 18th century

Ninny – foolish and weak person

Ninnyhammer flycatcher – an oaf

Nip Cheese – purser on a ship (pursers were renowned for stealing from seamen's allowances); also any stingy person

No better than they ought to be – worse than many

Noddiepeak slmpleton – an oaf

Noddy – simpleton, fool; also a type of buggy or one horse chaise

Noisome – smelly, noxious, disagreeable

Non-con – non comformist

Norfolk Howard – bed bug

Norway neckcloth – pillory (usually made with wood from Norwegian fir)

Nose and chin – gin (rhyming slang)

Nose-bagger – day visitor to the seaside who brings his own food (in a bag) and spends nothing locally

Nostrum – quack medicine

Not on borrowing terms – not friendly ('we're not on borrowing terms with the neighbours')

Not the cheese – unsatisfactory

Not today, Baker – no thank you

Not up to Dick – poorly

Not worth a rap – worthless

Notch – private parts of a woman

Now or never – clever

Nuf ced – no need to say more

Nug – word of endearment as in 'my dear nug'

Nugatory – trifling and pointless and without value

Numbskull – fool, idiot

Nummamorous – loving money

Nunnery – bawdy house

Nuptiated – married

Nurse the hoe-handle – lazy (about a gardener or farm labourer)

Nursery noodles – fastidious critics who pick fault with everything

Nuts – agreeable as in 'it was nuts for everyone' means 'everyone had a good time'

Nympholepsy – yearning for the impossible or unattainable; sometimes used to describe the passion of men for girls

Nypper – a cut purse; in 1585 a man called Wotton kept an academy in London where pick-pockets and cut purses were trained; since many people wore their purse on a belt or girdle the easiest way to steal it was to cut it; it seems possible that Wotton was the model for Fagin, the character in Charles Dickens' novel 'Oliver Twist'

O

Oaf – stupid, clumsy or boorish man

Oats – man who has sown his wild oats and is now staid and sober

Obliquity –a tendency towards the obscure or the unorthodox approach

Obloquy – public disgrace and condemnation; from late Middle English; in earlier centuries it might have led to a day in the stocks, these days it will probably lead to being 'cancelled' and banned

Obnubilate – to cover with fog or clouds

Obscurantist – someone who deliberately hides the truth

Odd job man – bit of a shyster, does a variety of things but none of them very well

Oddling – lonely, strange individual

Oenomel – drink made of wine and honey (from a very old, Greek recipe)

Oh chase me – a flirtatious invitation

Oh Willie, Willie – reproach, rather satirically intended, directed at a taradiddler

Old bean – friendly, informal form of address to a man (so old that the origin is long forgotten)

Old cloaks, suits or coats – this was another popular street cry which was heard in English cities and towns well into the second half of the twentieth century; rag and bone men used horse drawn carts to travel the streets buying unwanted clothes (and anything else) – it was the advent of charity shops which finally put them out of business

Old clock – wife (the term was used in Sterne's novel Tristram Shandy)

Old gang – old men

Old geyser – elderly man

Old Nick – the devil

Old put – pretentious, rather stupid old man

Old Roger – the devil

Old Toast – a brisk old fellow

Old Wigsby – narrow minded, bad tempered old man

Oldster – ageing man

Oleaginous – oily

Oligophageous – picky eater

Olio – miscellaneous collection of things

Oliver – fist (rhyming slang – from 'Oliver Twist')

Olla podrida – same as olio

On for a tatur – enraptured

On his feet – ruined

On the marry – looking for wife or husband

On the nail – immediate payment, no tick

On velvet – enjoying luxury

Once a week man (also Sunday promenader) – man in debt who can only go out on Sundays because on Sundays no arrests for debt could be made

One and a peppermint drop – one eyed person

One bites – small sour apples which are thrown away after one bite

One consecutive night – quite enough

One leg trouser – tight skirt

One light undershirt and no suspenders weather – very hot weather

One of us – a harlot; introduced as 'this is one of us' or 'this is one of my cousins'

Oniomania – compulsive buying disorder; an addiction to retail therapy

Onymous – bearing a name; the antonym of anonymous

Opprobious – expressing criticism or scorn

Opsimath – one who develops slowly and learns late in life

Orchidaceous – relating to a member of the orchid family of flowers

Order of the Boot – kick on the rear end

Otiose – useless, without purpose; most of the stuff manufactured, sold in extravagant packaging and specifically designed to be given as Christmas presents, to people you don't know very well, can safely be described as otiose ('Oh, thank you, another cigarette lighter designed as a model of Blackpool Tower; it will be invaluable if I ever take up smoking')

Ottoman – low, padded seat with a hinged lid and storage space beneath

Oubliette – secret dungeon, with access only through the ceiling; used for prisoners who could then be forgotten and pretty much ignored; a late 18th century word derived from the French word 'oublier' meaning to forget

Out of sorts – out of sorts of type (a problem faced by printers in the composing room)

Outward man – man who is rarely at home

Oven – big mouth

Oxymoron – figure of speech, with two contradictory terms used together e.g. honest politician, army intelligence, entertaining rapper

Oyster – gob of thick phlegm, coughed up by a person with consumption

P

Pabulum – bland or insipid entertainment (from the mid-17th century and invented by someone who foresaw television of the 21st century

Packet – false report

Packing-ken – restaurant, café

Pad – highway; a foot pad was a robber who operated on the highway

Padder – Paddington Station in London

Paint the town red – a dangerous, exciting evening out

Paladin – a knight, hero

Palimpsest – manuscript on which newer writing appears together with the original; anything reused which still bears signs of its earlier life or use (e.g. wine bottle used as a lamp but still bearing the original label)

Palinoia – need compulsively to repeat an action until it is done perfectly

Pallaver – flatter, talk

Palliards – beggars in patched cloaks

Panegyrise – speak or write in praise of

Panny – fight among women

Pantalettes – loose, divided drawers with frills at bottom of each leg

Pantler – butler

Pantywaist – effeminate or feeble

Parable – long, dreary, moralistic tale

Paradiddle – relatively recent word (coined in the 1920s) which defines a basic drumming pattern of 'left right, left left' or 'right left right right'. I have included it in this book as my solitary exception to the rules solely because it's a lovely looking word and a delight to say out loud and if the Victorians had thought of it they would have done so proudly.

Paradigm – a pattern or model

Paramour – lover, of the illicit variety; the illicit lover of a married person

Parish pick-axe – prominent nose

Parts his hair with a towel – bald (in use since 1882)

Passerine – birds which have feet adapted for perching

Patricoes – rogues

Paume – conceal in the hand as in 'he paumed a die' or 'he paumed the ace of hearts'

Peas in the pot – hot (rhyming slang)

Pecksniffian – hypocritical (from Mr Pecksniff in Dicken's Martin Chuzzlewit)

Pedlar's pony – walking stick

Peel the patch off the weak point – expose someone's weakness

Peen – curved, spherical or wedge shaped end of a hammer (as opposed to the bit used for knocking in nails)

Peeper – telescope or spy glass

Pego – penis

Peignoir – a negligee or light dressing gown (from the French word 'peigner', since this item of clothing was originally worn while a woman combed her hair); it is strangely satisfying to realise that there was once a time when women had a special item of clothing to wear when they were combing their hair

Pell-mell – jumbled together in a confusion

Pennorth of Treacle – charming girl

Penny gush – florid, purple prose written for London papers

Penny locket – pocket (rhyming slang)

Penny pick – cigar

Peregrinate – wander around, travel; from late 16th century (Middle English)

Perfect lady – anything but a perfect lady; woman drunk and misbehaving

Perfumed talk – bad language

Peripatetic – travelling from one place to another, usually to find work

Periwinkle – wig, penis or small mollusc; also means to winkle something out of someone (first used in various forms in the late 16th century)

Pernoctation – spending the night, early 17th century from the Latin pernoctare which means through the night

Persiflage –mocking banter

Petard – small bomb used, for example, to make a hole in a wall

Peter – portmanteau or cloke bag

Peter lay – stealing a portmanteau

Petit bleu – forgery

Petticoat pensioner – man kept by a woman for services rendered

Pheasant – dried herring

Philistines – bailiffs

Picayune – petty, insignificant

Picker-up – woman of the town

Pickthank – mischief maker or tale teller

Picture frame – gallows

Pidgin – mixture of two or three languages of which English is invariably one

Pieces – someone who is 'all to pieces' is exhausted

Pie shop – dog (from the assumption that penny pies were made with dog meat)

Piece – woman, wench; a good piece was a wench active and skilful in the art of amorous congress; in Cambridge there was a popular toast among university men which was 'May we never have a piece that will injure the constitution'

Pieuvre (though other spellings are possible) – prostitute (from Victor Hugo)

Pig in a poke – country folk who bought a piglet in a bag (or poke) were advised to look in the bag before handing over their money lest they discover later that they've purchased a bag containing something far less valuable than a small pig

Pig months – the eight months in which there is an 'r' and which, therefore, it is safest to eat pork

Pigeon – weak and silly fellow; a sucker

Pigeon pair – boy and girl children with the boy born first

Piglon – weak person, easily imposed upon

Pigot – lie

Pigsney – darling, sweetheart; used fondly as in 'will you be my pigsney?'

Pigtail – old man

Pilgarlic – bald man

Pill pusher – doctor (a piece of quiet abuse which became steadily more accurate through the years)

Pimp – male procurer

Pimp whiskin – a senior, well-established pimp

Pin money – amount of money given to a married woman for her personal, pocket expenses

Pince-nez – eyeglasses held in place solely by a nosepiece (there are no arms); the pince-nez may be attached to the owner's coat with a cord or gold chain

Pindle Smith – surgeon

Pint o'mahogany – coffee

Pintle – penis; an old English word; more recently used as a name for the pin on which a boat rudder turns

Pip pip – goodbye, or possibly a warning or possibly just a general purpose phrase a la 'oo la la'

Pitcher – a woman's private commodity

Plaister of warm guts – one warm belly clapped to another; this was a recipe popularly prescribed for a host of different disorders

Play consumption – malinger

Plenitudinous – copious, abundant

Plook – pimple or spot; originated in Middle English, probably from Scotland

Plug tail – penis

Pocket actor – small actor (and, oddly enough, you will be relieved to know that a pocket actress is a small actress though, of course, these days there are no actresses but just actors)

Poculation – drinking alcohol

Podsnappery – ignoring the inconvenient

Poetaster – someone who would like to be a poet but isn't quite; someone who writes distinctly second rate poetry

Poisoned – pregnant

Poke – purse

Poltroon – a coward

Pontius Pilate – pawnbroker

Poor man's goose – bullock's liver, served with sage and onions

Popinjay – someone vain and conceited; a popinjay usually dresses extravagantly and colourfully

Popinjay – vain, rather silly fool who is a bit of a dandy and dresses extravagantly; a Middle English word taken from the archaic word for a parrot, though parrots can be quite intelligent

Poppy cock – nonsense

Poppycock – gibberish, nonsense, balderdash; (the word, which first appeared in the 19th century) is derived from the Dutch word pappekak which is itself derived from two words 'pap' meaning 'soft' and 'kak' meaning 'dung')

Popsy wopsy – doll like girl

Pornocracy – government by prostitutes; the word dates back to 19th century

Porridge hole –mouth

Portable property – anything easily stolen and pawned

Postman's sister – secret informant

Pot o'bliss – good looking, tall woman

Potsheen – whisky

Poultice – fat woman

Powder monkey – boy on a ship of war whose job it is to fetch powder from the magazine

Powdering his hair – getting drunk

Prancer – horse

Prating – talking foolishly, or boringly and at great length

Prattling box – pulpit

Pratts – buttocks

Prawn – term of endearment as in 'I expect you're a saucy young prawn'

Prester John – the unknown

Pretty – gallant, alert fellow, prompt and ready

Pretty steep – threatening

Prey – money

Prig – self-righteous person who acts as though they are superior to everyone else; first used in this sense in the middle of the 16th century, before that it meant a thief, and a prig-napper was a thief taker

Priggers or prancers – horse thieves

Prigstar – rival in love

Prinking – dressing up smartly as in 'she spent an hour prinking before dinner'

Prittle Prattle – gossip, pointless chatter

Prize faggots – well-developed breasts

Procacity – insolence

Procerity – height, tallness

Process pusher – lawyer's clerk

Prodonna – professional lady, actress with profitable sideline

Professional beauty – society woman who is photographed a good deal

Prognathous – projecting lower jaw or chin

Proper bit of frock – pretty, well dressed girl

Proud – wanting sex or, as James Caulfield put it in 1793 'desirous of copulation'

Pucker water – water containing alum which was used to counterfeit virginity

Puddings – intestines, as in 'if you say that again I'll put a knife to your belly and let out your puddings'

Puff guts – fat man

Pulchritudinous – comely

Pull down the blind – suggestion to young couple being amorous in public

Pull down your basque – behave yourself (to a woman)

Pull the string proper – manipulate the public (taken from manipulating marionettes)

Pully Hawley – romping, as in 'they were having a game of Pully Hawley and didn't hear the door open'

Punch – alcohol in a form regarded as confusing outside England because it contained water to make it weak, spirits to make it strong, lemon juice to make it sour and sugar to make it sweet; served at parties, balls, celebrations and so on.

Punchable wench – girl ripe for a man

Punk – whore or a soldier's trull

Purdonium – a coal scuttle

Purse proud – person who is vain about their wealth

Pushing school – brothel

Put a steam on the table – earn enough to pay for a hot Sunday dinner

Put his light out – kill him

Put on the pot – be rather grand

Put to bed – conquer

Put your clothes together when you come – come for a long visit

Q

Quack – uneducated, unqualified, ignorant, fake medical practitioner; a vendor of nostrums; now commonly found on YouTube (a forum where the ignorant teach the gullible everything they know about nothing much but do so with the brash confidence only the completely uninformed can muster)

Quacksalver – quack; someone who boasts about, and probably offers for sale, their self-proclaimed medical skills and nostrums; from the 17th century and probably derived from a Dutch word meaning prattle

Quakebuttock – coward

Quarter stretch – three months imprisonment

Quartern o'bliss – small woman

Quean – slut

Queen Street – a man governed by his wife is said to live in Queen Street

Queen's weather – sunshine (throughout her reign Queen Victoria almost always had lovely weather whenever she had a public engagement)

Queer – bad, worthless fellow

Queer as Dick's hatband – out of order

Queer plunger – confidence trickster who specialises in 'falling' into water (usually in the form of a pond or slow moving river) and being rescued by their accomplices; they are then taken into one of the nearby houses appointed by the Humane Society for the recovery of drowned persons. And there they are rewarded with a guinea each. The rescued person, who usually claims he was driven to attempting suicide by terrible circumstances, will usually also receive money.

Queer shovers – people who circulate bad money

Querimony – complaint

Quiddity – a distinctive feature or pecularity

Quidnunc – inquisitive and gossipy person

Quids – money

Quiffing – rogering

Quill driver – clerk

Quim – the part of the female body likely to be decorated with a merkin; defined in one very early dictionary as 'a piece's furbelow'

Quire – rogue who has sung in several choirs (a choir is a synonym for gaol)

Quisquous – puzzling

Quiz – odd looking fellow

Quod – prison

Quotidian – daily

R

Rabbit – bread and cheese toasted, known as Welch rare bit; rabbits were also wooden vessels to drink from

Rabbit catcher – midwife

Rabbit sucker – young spendthrift, buying goods on tick

Rabelasian – bawdy, earthy humour

Rag – mess around with someone's furniture but without doing any damage (students at university)

Ragamuffin – ragged person; aka a tatterdemallion

Rags – lower class London newspapers (today, this would include broadsheets as well as red top tabloids)

Railway bible – pack of playing cards

Railways – red stockings

Rain-napper – umbrella

Raked fore and aft – head over heels in love

Raker – comb

Ralph Spooner – fool

Rampallian – wanton woman; good for nothing slut

Randle – set of nonsensical verses which had to be repeated by those who had farted; anyone who failed to randle successfully was liable to be kicked and pinched

Rantallion – man whose scrotum is so relaxed that it is longer than his penis

Rantipole – rude, romping boy or girl; a gadabout; someone dissipated

Rascal – cheeky or mischievous man or boy; originally a rascal was a man without genitals (possibly from the Italian word rascaglione meaning a eunuch); if a woman called a man a rascal the vulgar response was (according to 'Blackguardiana') 'the offer of an ocular demonstration of the virility of the party so defamed'

Rational costume – trousers worn by women

Rattler – coach and horses as in 'the 4.15 rattler is running three days late'

Rattling cove – coachman

Readied the rosser – bribed the police

Rebarbative – unattractive and objectionable; from late 19th century

Red herring – deliberate deceit

Red hot treat – dangerous person

Red letter day – saint's day or holiday, marked on the calendars in red

Red rag – tongue (advice to an over-talkative person might be 'shut your potato trap and give your red rag a holiday')

Redding up – tidying the house

Redundant – impudent

Rejectamenta – things discarded or rejected as useless e.g. most things bought in the sales

Rep – woman of reputation (this does not mean that she was of great intellect, achievement or artistic talent)

Resurrection men – people employed by anatomy students to steal dead bodies out of churchyards so that they could be dissected in anatomy classes

Reversed – man held upside down by bullies so that his money fell out of breeches and landed on the ground, the bullies would kindly pick up the fallen money

Rhino – money

Ribbaldry – vulgar abuse

Ribbalds – originally ribbalds were mercenary soldiers who travelled about serving any master who paid them but eventually the word came to refer to common bandits

Rich face – red, pimpled face

Ridge – guinea (twenty one shillings in old English money)

Riding St George – amorous congress with the woman uppermost

Riff raff – low, vulgar people (from the French rif et raf)

Right ho! – jolly greeting favoured by upper class twits and immortalised by P.G.Wodehouse in his books about Bertie Wooster and his manservant Jeeves.

Ripper – murderer of women

Risky – cautious and scrupulous adultery

Road starver – long coat made without pockets so that there is nothing for a highwayman or pick pocket to steal (and nothing for a beggar)

Roaring trade – brisk trade

Roast meat clothes – Sunday or holiday best

Robbing the barber – wearing long hair

Robert's men – thieves in the style of Robin Hood

Roger – a portmanteau but as a verb to roger was to make love to someone (usually, in pre-emancipation days, a man rogered a woman rather than the other way round)

Rogue – dishonest person

Roly poly – round, plump person

Romp – a forward, wanton girl

Rook – to swindle or cheat; also a bird, member of the corvid family, similar to the crow

Rooms – a woman who was known to let out her fore room and lay backwards was a prostitute

Rorty bloke – damned fine fellow, trustworthy

Rotten orange – term of contempt (dates back to William III – Prince of Orange, who wasn't enormously popular)

Rough – to sleep in your clothes was to rough it

Rough music – banging of pans and pots, marrow bones and cleavers; rough music was produced when a village wanted to express its disapproval of an individual, a couple or a family

Rovers – pirates, vagabonds

Rubbish – luggage

Ruffle – someone pretending to be an old soldier etc., usually for pecuniary benefit (naturally, the ruffle, hasn't been anywhere near a battlefield or a weapon)

Rugose – wrinkled, corrugated, as in 'Dear Mrs P, you have a beautifully rugose complexion'

Rum beck – justice of the peace

Rum blower – good looking wench

Rum cull – rich fool, easily cheated

Rum doxy – fine wench

Rum dubber – thief who picks locks expertly

Rum duke – jolly and handsome fellow

Rum kicks – breeches decorated or laced with gold or silver brocade

Rum padders – highwaymen, well-armed and on good horses

Rum rigging – smart clothes

Rum topping – rich commode

Rump and kidney men – fiddlers who play at feasts, fairs and weddings; part of their payment would be to eat up the leftovers

Runner – dog stealer

Running stationers – hawkers selling newspapers and pamphlets containing details of trials and speeches made by men about to die on the gallows (these publications were enormously popular)

Runt – short, squat man or woman (sometimes known as Welsh runts)

Rushers – thieves who knock at the door of a big house in London during the summer when the family is out of town (in their country house); when the door was opened by a servant, the 'rushers' would rush in and steal the contents

Rusted in – settled down, comfortable

Rutting – copulating, both of animals and humans

S

Sad, bad and mad – fashionable lamentations

Sack – pocket; and so 'to dive into the sack' means 'to pick a pocket'

Sad dog – wicked, debauched fellow; Jonathan Swift (the author of Gulliver's Travels) preferred the Latin 'tristis canis'

Saddling paddock – place of assignation

St John's Wood donas – better class prostitute (usually living in St John's Wood)

St Lubbock – orgy or drunken riot

Sal hatch – dirty wench

Sal slappers – common woman

Sally – tall, thin woman in evening dress

Sally Lunn – Chelsea bun

Salt – lecherous person, bitch in heat

Same old 3 and 4 – a wage of 3 shillings and 4 pence a day would, after six working days, give a weekly wage of £1

Sandwich – food (originally meat but later pretty well anything edible) placed between two slices of bread. The sandwich was invented by the fourth earl of Sandwich in the 18th century. He liked gambling so much that he didn't want to leave the gambling table to eat. So he had the club staff put a piece of meat between two hunks of bread and thereby immortalised himself and his family

Sans-culottes – poorly clothed man (not necessarily without knee length breeches)

Sapid – lively, tasty, interesting (from the 17th century and originally from the Latin sapere which means 'to taste')

Saporous – tasty (a good word to use at dinner parties – as in 'this is extremely saporous, Annabella')

Sasha – to dance, slip or slide from side to side

Satrap – petty despot; the world is full of them though they do seem to congregate in planning departments, Post Offices and banks

Saturday pie – pie containing the week's unwanted leftovers

Scab – worthless man or woman

Scaffold pole – fried potato chip, sold with fried fish in 19th century

Scalper – merciless in financial dealings

Scamp – highwayman who is polite as he goes about his work

Scandal-broth – tea (because scandals are often shared while drinking the stuff)

Scape-gallows – someone who deserved to hang but didn't

Scobberlotcher – idler

Scoffing – mocking or ridiculing someone or something

Sconce – the head

Scoundrel – man without principles

Scrap – villainous scheme

Scraper – fiddler

Screamer – alarmist article written to attract attention

Scrip – any scrap or slip of paper

Scrofulous – infected, or appearing to be infected, with scrofulous (tuberculosis outside the lungs)

Scrub – low, mean sort of fellow who does all sorts of dirty work

Scurryfunge – an old fashioned toothbrush, stiff hooked article

Scuttler – young street rough

Sea side moths – bed bugs

Second hand woman – widow

Send off – article, story or poem designed to attract attention

Sentimental hairpin – insignificant girl

Seraglio – bawdy house (from the name of the great Turk's palace, wherein many women were kept)

Sesquipedalian – someone who uses long, polysyllabic words (usually when short ones will do very nicely)

Settle – to knock someone down and so 'we settled the cull by a stoter on his nob' means we stunned the bloke with a blow on his head'

Shadder – thin, worn out person

Shag bag – a mean, poor, sneak of a fellow; a man of no spirit

Shandygaff – shandy (originated in late 19th century so as words go this one is a baby)

Shant of bivvy – pint of beer

She-male – transgendered female

She napper – female thief catcher

Sheriff's Ball – execution

Sheriff's Bracelets – handcuffs

Shibboleth – long standing belief or principle, now regarded as out of date or outmoded (popular in the 17th century (political parties always use the word to describe the manifestos of their opponents and they are generally justified in this)

Shift – straight chemise or slip which has no waist

Shill – confidence trickster's accomplice

Shillelagh – knobbed stick, carried and used for defence and attack

Shimmy – archaic term for chemise

Shipwrecked – drunk

Shoot the cat – to vomit

Shoot your cuff – make yourself look as good as you can

Shoulder clapper – someone who claps you on the shoulder in a sign of great familiarity, but usually does so dishonestly or with some ulterior motive, feigning friendship; of course, some shoulder-clappers are just chums (usually male) who haven't seen you for five minutes and who have had too much to drink

Shoulder tapper – bailiff

Showy – overdressed, over made-up

Shrapnel – fragments from a bomb or mine; the word comes from an English artillery officer called Henry Shrapnel

Shy cock – someone who stays indoors to avoid the bailiffs

Sick in 14 languages – very poorly

Sign of a house to let – widow's weeds

Signed all over – a good painting is said to be 'signed all over' if the identity of the artist is immediately apparent

Silly dinner – free feast

Silly moo – daft woman

Silver streak – English Channel

Simkin – foolish fellow

Simnel – two kinds of cake baked as one (originally the result of an accident in the kitchen)

Simpleton – foolish fellow

Sir Timothy – someone who wants to be the big cheese and therefore makes a big fuss of paying the bill for a group of people in a pub or restaurant

Sissies – effeminate men

Sitting breeches – someone who stays late is said to be wearing his sitting breeches

Six pounder – maid servant (the wage once given to maid servants was six pounds that's six pounds a year, not six pounds a month, a week or an hour)

Skilamalink – secret and rather shady

Skinners – mental torture (from the physical torture of being flayed alive)

Skulker – soldier who feigns sickness to avoid his duty; outside the military it refers to anyone who keeps out of the way when there is work to be done

Sky farmers – tricksters who claimed that they were farmers on the Isle of Skye (or somewhere else remote) and that because of a flood or a hurricane or a tsunami or some other natural disaster they lost everything: 'and if you could see your way to sparing a shilling, sir…'

Sky parlour – garret

Slabberdegullion – worthless slob, careless or slovenly person (according to the OED this word has not been used since the 16th century but I have used it this century in a published work (not this one) and, since it is one of my favourite words, I intend to make sure I use it again before long); alternative form is 'slubber de gullion'

Slaister – to slap on make-up, as a vamp might do

Slammerkin – slattern, and the loose covering she may wear

Slap – theatre make up

Slated – patient is about to die (at the London Hospital in the 19th century, friends and relatives of patients were only allowed to visit patients who were dying and whose names had been written on the porter's slate)

Slattern – a woman who dresses badly and who looks like a slut

Sling a slobber – blow a kiss

Sling your hook – be fired (taken from coal mines where miners hung their bag in the dressing room – when they were fired they took their bag off the hook and left)

Slip – a petticoat, usually a short one

Slipgibbet –someone who deserved to hang but didn't

Sloomy – spiritless and dull

Slops – clothes and bedding used by seamen

Slosh the brick – beat the wife

Slosh the old gooseberry – beat the wife

Slush bucket – someone who eats a great deal of greasy food

Slut – promiscuous or slovenly woman

Slutchy – muddy

Sly boots – cunning fellow, but one who pretends to be a simple chap

Small coals – small coal was sold door to door from 1625 in London; men would cry out 'small coals!' while carrying a supply of coal in a sack on his back; in the 17th century coal was sold at a penny a peck; when I was a small boy, my parents had coal delivered regularly – men covered in coal dust from head to toe would carry sacks of coal on their shoulders down a longish driveway, through the garage and conservatory, down a long flight of steps and into the coal store (I rather think it cost more than a penny a peck)

Smeech – smoke, from a fire

Smoker – club or concert where there was much singing, smoking and telling of stories

Smothering a parrot – drinking a glass of absinthe neat

Snap your head off – brusque

Snappy – attractive (about a person or a thing)

Snide-sparkler – false diamond

Snudge – noun (miser) or verb (to hoard)

Soap – girls

Society maddists – people who spend their lives fighting to climb into a higher echelon of society

Socket money – fee paid to a whore

Soldier's supper – nothing at all to eat

Solecism – poor behaviour, poor manners or faulty grammatical style

Solipsism – selfishness, being self-centred; being convinced that nothing and no one else exists; motorists who carelessly park across two spaces in a crowded car park are solipsists

Solo player – someone who plays a musical instrument so badly that no one will stay in the same room

Something in the city – dismissive judgement of someone's occupation; probably not as important as it has been made to sound

Sooterkin – it is said that Dutch women put stoves under their petticoats and bred small furry animals called sooterkins (this was apparently considered quite a good joke back in the 18th century, and possibly earlier, but today it seems quite insane – but then so does much of what passes for entertainment these days so who are we to judge?)

Sossidge-slump – failure, from 'sossidge', meaning failure in German (the phrase originated when the Emperor of Germany sent a telegram to President Kruger congratulating him on repulsing Dr

Jameson's raid. The telegram made Germany unpopular and German imports collapsed dramatically as a result.)

Soubrette – female singer, opera style

Soubriquet – nickname

Soul doctor – parson

Soul driver – parson

Sow – fat woman

Spanish sweat – the pox; venereal disease

Spanish worm – a nail, or more specifically, a nail which appears in a board which is being sawn

Spanks or spankers – money

Spark – fashionable man

Sparrer – items found in dustbins (from bin diving)

Spatchcock – hen killed and immediately skinned and broiled, but spatchcock also means to add something inappropriate (a phrase or sentence) to a document (from the 18th century)

Spawling – a noisy clearing of the throat

Speak – to court or make love to someone

Speak with – to rob

Spin – spinster (boatloads of spins travelled to India in search of husbands)

Spindle-shanks – a person with long thin legs

Spit amber – expectorate while chewing tobacco

Spitchcock – split and grill or fry an eel

Spoonerism – verbal transposition, producing a comedic effect; invented accidentally by Rev William Spooner

Spooning the brick – making love to the wife of a friend

Spoony stuff – sentimental and contemptible play or book

Squealer – informer

Squire of Alsatia – spendthrift, profligate person who likes to be seen as the squire or leader of a company

Squirt – doctor

Stallion – man kept by an old lady for providing personal services

Star gazer – hedge whore

Start a jolly – lead the applause in a theatre

State – a man was said to be lying in state if he was in bed with three harlots

Stays – metal, wood, whalebone rods between layers of stiffened linen and fastened with lacings; worn over a chemise to pull in waist and give more shape. The wearer of a corset could hardly breathe or speak. The invention of the metal eyelet hole in 1828 made it possible to lace tighter and make waists smaller, whalebone eventually took over from iron and wood and as a result the whaling industry boomed.

Steal someone's thunder – help yourself to another person's idea or work without giving credit or recompense (this phrase originated in the 17th century when a playwright called John Dennis invented stage thunder for a play he had written; when his play failed his fake thunder was stolen for someone else's play and Dennis stood up and cried out: 'They won't act my piece, but they steal my thunder'.)

Steatopygous – very large bottom; an extremely popular characteristic in some communities

Stewed quaker – drink consisting of burned rum with a little butter melted in it

Stick and bangers – billiard cue and balls; also has a more personal meaning

Stitch – nickname for a tailor

Stock jobbers – people who gamble on public funds but only bet on certainties and even so do not have sufficient funds to make good the payments for which they are contracted

Stockings – garment, usually made of silk or wool, which covers the foot and leg and is held up by a suspender belt or a garter; worn by both sexes

Stoter – blow

Straight as they make 'em – honest

Strapping – lying with a woman

Stretching – hanging

Strike a bargain – two people making an agreement hit the butt ends of their riding whips together; this was the 18th century equivalent of the Roman habit of a buyer and seller exchanging straws to confirm a bargain

Striker – watch (usually one which made a pleasant sound, or even played a tune, at the top of the hour, etc.)

Strum – periwig; very large wig; as a verb to strum was to have carnal knowledge of a woman or to play badly on any stringed instrument, though presumably not at the same time

Strumpet – prostitute or promiscuous woman; Middle English

Stuck up – broke (after you've been stuck up by a highwayman you won't have any money and you'll be broke)

Subderisorius – quiet but affectionate ridicule; gently mocking; according to the Oxford English Dictionary this word was last used in 1668 by a man called Henry More who was a poet and philosopher

Succedaneum – a substitute

Suggilate – beat until bruised

Susurrant – whispering or rustling or humming softly; first appeared in the 19th century

Swag – shop

Sweetheart – word to show great affection, originated in 13th century when it was two words

Sweating – reducing the weight of a gold coin and stealing the reduction; according to the dictionary 'Blackguardiana' this practice was chiefly favoured by Jews; sweating was also the name given to a sport practised by young bloods in the 17th century – the bloods would lie in wait and surprise an innocent passer-by; they would surround him and then use their swords to prick him on the posterior, constantly turning him round until they considered him to be sufficiently sweated

Swell – an upper class individual

Swigmen – thieves who travel the country buying old shoes and old clothes and selling brooms and mops, but who make most of their money by stealing

Swipe – steal (men wore silk pocket handkerchiefs called 'wipes' which were worth stealing, and stealing a wipe became known as to swipe – cf Fagin and the Artful Dodger in Oliver Twist)

Syntax – schoolmaster

T

Tab – to enjoy a tab was to enjoy a day of pleasure with wife and family

Tabby – old maid

Table beer – cheap, poor beer

Tabs – older women (because tabby cats were always associated with older women)

Tackle – mistress ('the cull tipt his tackle rum rigging' means that the man bought his mistress good clothes)

Tag, rag and bobtail – mixture of 'low' people who follow one another just as St Anthony was followed by his pig

Tailor's goose – an iron used by tailors to press down seams

Take gruel – to die (anyone drinking gruel was probably dying)

Take gruel together – to live together as man and wife even if not married

Take it lying down – cowardly (a man would stand up)

Take the egg – win

Tale bearers – mischief makers

Tale tellers – people hired to tell stories

Tally men – brokers that rent out clothes to women of the town

Tallywags – testicles

Tap – gentle touch on the shoulder from a bailiff

Taradiddle – a trifling falsehood

Tart – girl, prostitute, young woman accurately described as 'no better than she ought to be'

Tatler – watch

Tats – false dice

Tatterdemalion – as an adjective tattered or dilapidated; as a noun someone wearing tattered clothes; first commonly used in the early 17th century

Tax fencer – crooked shopkeeper

Tayle drawers – thieves who steal gentlemen's swords from their sides

Tea in a mug – anyone drinking tea in a mug was thought to have poor breeding and so 'he's the sort who drinks tea in a mug'

Tea voider – chamber pot

Teddy my Godson – a simple minded fellow as in 'this is Teddy my Godson'

Temulence – drunkenness; (this book is full of synonyms for drunk and drunkenness but this is merely a reflection of the language used in earlier centuries)

Tender Parnell – fearful person, so anxious and nervous that a leaf rustling will cause consternation

That won't pay the old woman her ninepence – condemn an act of evasion or financial crookery

That's the ticket – the right thing to do ('ticket' is taken from old French; the rules of behaviour or etiquette were written on cards known as tickets)

The game's afoot – taken from Shakespeare. P.G.Wodehouse, the English humourist related that he once met Arthur Conan Doyle hurrying along a street in New York. Doyle breathlessly explained that he was hot on the foot of book pirates who had stolen some of his work and published it without paying royalties. 'The game's afoot!', said Doyle as he hurried off. I like the phrase so much I used it as a title for one of my volumes of diaries.

Then the band played – climax; political candidates would employ a brass band to strike up when their opponent tried to speak

Theomania – condition in which an individual thinks he is God; commoner than you might suppose and particularly common among those in positions of minor authority

Thief taker – individual who associates with criminals in order to betray them to the authorities and to then receive a reward (known as blood money)

Thieves' kitchen – London's new Law Courts

Thin as a rasher of wind – very thin man

Thingembob – name for anything unmentionable or anything for which the proper term has been forgotten

Thirteenth juryman – bent or prejudiced judge

Thorn-back – old maid

Thorough cough – coughing and breaking wind backwards at the same time

Thoroughly good natured wench – one who, when asked to sit down, will lie down

Three legged mare (or stool) – gallows

Thribble – making do and muddling through

Thrung – packed or cluttered

Thumper – confidence trickster who steals by telling thumpers (big lies)

Thwack – a heavy blow

Tib – young girl

Tib of the buttery – goose (the bird not the action)

Tick – take goods upon trust

Ticket skinner – someone who buys and sells theatre or opera tickets to make a profit

Tickrum – licence (licences were rare items in the era to which this book relates, today you can't sneeze without the appropriate tickrum)

Tiddle – to fidget with or cosset

Tiffing – eating or drinking outside meal times; snacking or grazing

Tight as a boiled owl – drunk

Tin – money

Tip – give or lend

Tip the velvet – kiss with the tip of the tongue

Tip top – the best

Tiring – dressing (probably because women used to wear a great many clothes, and dressing used to involve a good many bows and laces)

Tit – a horse

Tit for tat – to give as good as he gets (popular in the 16th century but then it was known as 'tip for tap' – just why the change took place is one of life's small mysteries)

Titivil – a knave or a trivial piece of gossip

Titotular bosh – complete nonsense

Titter tatter – sea saw

Tittle tattle – idle chit chat, gossip; in use since the early 16th century

Tittup – someone with a mincing, prancing gait; tittuping girls

Titular – formal position which gives the holder authority solely through their title so, for example, the King of England has status and authority only because he happens to be the King

Toad eater – poor female relation; reduced gentlewoman; the name comes from the fact that doctors used to do their experiments on their servants, and one experiment so conducted was making the servant swallow a supposedly poisonous toad to see what happened

Toad in the hole – meat baked or boiled in a pie crust

Toast – drinking to good health; the custom was said to have originated when a beautiful woman was found bathing in a cold bath and one of her admirers, out of gallantry, drank some of the bath water, though just how this helped has never been made clear

Toasting iron – sword

Toe rag – beggar or footpad (since both walk, rather than ride, and are usually dressed in rags)

Toilet – originally, a cloth used for wrapping clothes, or towel placed around the shoulders by a barber, then the linen covering of a dressing table, then the table and stuff on it , make up, etc., and then in America, used it as a term for a water closet or lavatory

Token – plague or a venereal disease; the phrase 'she tipped him the token' translates as 'she gave him the pox'

Tom Turd Man – night man who empties the necessary containers from private houses

Tomnoddy – stupid or foolish person

Toodle-pip (also toodle-oo) – goodbye, see you soon

Tool – someone used by another as an instrument; also known as a cat's paw

Toothsome –voluptuous and alluring

Topping cove – hangman

Topsy Turvy – the top side the other way

Toralium – eiderdown

Toss pot – drunkard

Totty all colours – young woman in very colourful clothes

Totty headed – hare brained

Tout – lookout for criminals

Tra la la – goodbye, toodle pip

Trailing his coat – defiance (in villages in Ireland a man challenging another to a fight would trail his coat; if his prospective opponent trod on the coat then a fight would ensue)

Transmigrify (or transmography) – patch up or alter

Trapes – slatternly, sluttish woman

Travelling piquet – game played by travellers in a carriage; the players would look out of the window on their side of the carriage and score points as follows: A parson riding a grey horse (wins the game outright); an old woman under a hedge (wins the game outright); cat looking out of a window – 60 points; man, woman and a child in a buggy – 40 points; man with a woman walking behind him – 30 points; flock of sheep – 20 points; flock of geese – 20 points; a post chaise – 5 points; a man on a horse – 2 points; a man or woman walking – 1 point

Treacle-man – pretty male decoy would pretend to be the suitor of a housemaid and thereby gain access to a house for his companions to burgle; also used to describe commercial travellers selling sewing machines, etc., to young girls and old women

Tremulous – shaking or quivering

Trenchant – sharp and unusually vigorous in style and expression

Tretis – well-proportioned and graceful

Tripe – guts; and so 'Mr Double Trip(e)' refers to a fat man

Troll – loiter or saunter about

Trollop – lusty, coarse, sluttish woman

Trollope – loose garment, a carelessly worn and revealing wrap worn by a trollop, eventually became suitable for Sunday-go-to-meeting wear

Trull – prostitute; early 16th century from German word 'trulle'

Trying it on the dog – testing something; originally the idea was to give a small portion of a new foodstuff, or a present of foodstuff, to the dog to see if it became ill; and then in 19th century theatrical circles, new plays or musical recitals were tested by performing them before a matinee audience and that was known as 'trying it on the dog'

Tup running – this was the 18th equivalent of social media activities and was a highpoint at wakes and fairs in Derbyshire; a ram's tail was soaped and greased and the animal was then allowed to run among the multitude; anyone who could catch the ram by the tail and hold onto him could keep him. (This gay sport was also played with a pig as the starring attraction and it was, no doubt, far more entertaining than an hour spent updating a Facebook account.)

Turdiform – having the appearance of a thrush; first used by a Mr Sharp in 1879 (Mr Sharp was a museum curator and ornithologist and either had a great sense of mischief or no sense of fun whatsoever)

Tureen – deep, covered dish usually for bringing soup or stew to the table

Turf – prostitution, taken from the observation that loose women tended to parade themselves for inspection (as horses are paraded before the punters)

Turn a blind eye – Admiral Nelson disagreed with orders he was given at the Battle of Copenhagen, and so when he looked at the signal flags he put his telescope to his blind eye

Turn over – article which requires readers to turn over the page to continue reading; a single column article on the right hand edge of the front page of a newspaper was usually a 'turn over'

Turn the tap on – cry; common in theatrical circles among actresses wanting to arouse sympathy in the audience after a sad song

Turnip pate – blond man

Turtle soup – broth made with a sheep's head

Tweedle-dum-sirs – knights (such as Sir Arthur Sullivan) who acquired their titles through their music

Twiddle diddles – testicles

Twit – to twit someone is to reproach them or to remind them of past favours conferred

Two handed – a big strapping man or woman can be described as 'two handed'

Two to one shop – pawnbrokers (the odds are two to one that the goods pledged will never be redeemed)

U

Ugly – thick

Ullage – the amount by which a container fails to be full, either through evaporation or leakage or the failure of the landlord or barmaid to provide full measure

Ultracrepidarian – someone who knows nothing about a subject but talks or writes extensively and with apparent confidence (today, broadsheet leader writers, talking heads on television and political advisors can be accurately described as ultracrepidarians)

Umper – original of umpire or referee

Uncumber – disencumber (St Uncumber – was a bearded woman and benefactress of wives, according to Sir Thomas More; it was said that for a peck of oats she would provide a horse upon which an evil husband could be constrained to ride to the devil – and so the dissatisfied wife could thus disencumber herself)

Understrapper – inferior in any office

Unfortunate women – prostitutes

Unicorn – coach drawn by three horses

Up a tree for tenpence – stony broke

Up the pole – drunk

Up to the scratch – fit for the job; believed to have originated with a lady committee going through lists of names to see which could be considered socially acceptable; the names which passed muster were marked with the scratch of a pen

Upper Benjamin – greatcoat

Upping block – steps for mounting a horse

Upright man – top rogue; in a gang or 'crew' of crooks, one man would be the 'upright man'; the nastiest, biggest rogue would be chosen for this post and he would have the right to sleep with new dells before anyone else in the fraternity; the upright man carried a truncheon called a filchman and he took a bigger share of the booty than anyone else in the gang; most gangs contained thirty to forty members (male and female) and the upright man's rule was absolute (until someone with a bigger filchman beat him to a pulp and took over the gang)

Urinal of the planets – Ireland, where it rains a good deal

Usher – sodomite

Usquebaugh (also usky) – whisky

Usufruct – the right to use someone else's property (but without damaging it)

Uxorious – man with great affection for his wife

V

Vagabond – homeless, jobless wanderer; a tramp

Vail – to take off a hat

Valentine – the first man seen by a woman, or woman seen by a man, on St Valentine's Day; it used to be said that birds chose their mate for the coming year on 14th February

Vamp – a woman who blatantly uses sexual attraction to take advantage of men; also 'to vamp' is 'to pawn'

Vampers – stockings

Vapours – supposedly vapours were exhalations of the organs rising to affect the brain and agitate the nervous system

Vapulation – beating or flogging

Varlet – scoundrel; unprincipled rogue; dates from 16th century; the word developed into 'valet', a male servant

Vaulting school – bawdy house

Vecordy – insanity, mental illness (according to the OED this word was only ever used in 1656, by a man called Thomas Blount who was apparently an antiquary and lexicographer; I have included it here in the hope that someone will use it again soon before it goes out of fashion and becomes as passé as platform shoes and turn-ups on trousers)

Venecund – shy and bashful

Veneration – respect, admiration

Ventripotent – having a large abdomen, giving the owner the appearance of a woman with an 18 month pregnancy

Venture girl – young lady who goes out to India in search of a husband

Venust – beautiful and elegant

Victualling office – the stomach

Vilipend – to hold cheap or think poorly of someone

Village blacksmith – a failure; an artiste who is never hired for more than a week at a time (seems rather unfair to real blacksmiths)

Virago – fierce, angry, brawling, violent, bad tempered woman (Old English)

Virginal – early spinet, with strings parallel to the keyboard, which was popular in 16th and 17th century England (as you know a spinet is a small piano or harpsichord)

Virgins' bus – last bus going west from Piccadilly in central London; named after the alleged nature of the majority of the female passengers who were returning home disappointed

Viritoot – a spree or jaunt or jolly time had by all

Vowel – to not pay money lost gambling; this comes from the loser repeating the vowels IOU in the continued hope that they will be accepted

W

Wabbler – pedestrian

Wagtail – lewd woman

Waits – musicians who play under the windows of better off house owners just before Christmas, in hope of receiving a Christmas box; these musicians are called 'waits' because they do a lot of waiting

Wake – country feast on the anniversary of the saint day of the village (that is the saint to which the parish church is dedicated – where local churches were named All Saints the locals must have enjoyed many feasts)

Walk out – failure (from the habit of theatrical audiences in America of walking out before the end of a theatrical performance they did not enjoy)

Walking the plank – mutineers blindfolded loyal officers and men and forced them to walk a plank laid over the ship's side; they did this believing that they would escape a charge of murder if they were caught

Walking mort – female vagabond

Walking poulterer – someone who steals hens and sells them from door to door

Walking Stationer – a hawker of pamphlets

Walking up the wall – run up a bill in an alehouse; bills are recorded by writing sums in chalk on the wall of the bar

Walled – a picture accepted for an exhibition was said to be 'walled'

Wanhope – despair

Wanton – ungoverned, rebellious

Wap – to wap is to copulate (there used to be an apparently unending number of synonyms for this activity)

Ware – a woman's ware; her 'commodity'

Warm – rich

Warm bit – a lively and vigorous woman

Warming pan – old fashioned watch

Warrocks – beware (probably taken from 'war hawks' which is a corruption of 'tomahawks' – the word originated in America)

Waspish – peevish, sharp

Water headed – someone who cries easily

Wattle – fleshy lobe hanging from neck

Way of all flesh – dead

Wee wees – Frenchmen (taken from the word 'oui')

Welcher – cheat (a bookmaker who doesn't pay up after a race is a 'welcher' and likely to have his clothes torn from his back so that he goes home with nothing)

Welkin – the sky, heaven

Well hung – man with exceptionally large genitals

Well set up – a bride with a handsome dowry

Well shod – well off

Wellingtons – rubber boots, named for the Duke of Wellington who wore long, black leather boots which bear no resemblance to modern wellingtons (I suspect he wouldn't have been seen dead wearing them)

Welsh Ejectment – taking the roof off a house; method used by Welsh landlords to get rid of unwanted tenants

Welsh mile (or Welch mile) – long and tedious as in 'he tells stories like Welsh miles'

Wet bobs – school or college students keen on boating (as opposed to dry bobs who were keen on cricket)

What! – exclamation of surprise, often tinged with disapproval

What ho! – upper class greeting made famous by Bertie Wooster in the comic novels by P.G.Wodehouse

What Paddy gave the drum – a thrashing

What would Mrs Boston say? – Boston was regarded by Americans as a rather superior, snobbish sort of place

What's that got to do with the price of fish? – what's the relevance of that? (This is my favourite English idiom. I was once thrilled to hear a man say this to his wife. He managed to get just the right amount of incredulity into his voice.)

Wheeze – jokes or gags in a play or music hall entertainment

Whet – first drink of the day, commonly a mug of white wine

Whiddle – preach or tell

Whiddler – informer or sneak

Whip the cock – sport practised at fairs, wakes and horse races in Leicestershire. A cock is tied into a hat and half a dozen carters are blindfolded and placed around it. The carters have their whips, and after being turned around three times they are invited to try to whip the cock. The first man to make the cock cry out keeps the cock. Of course, since they have been turned around three times, the men spend much of their time flogging each other. **Whippersnapper** – inexperienced, knowing little, but confident and presumptuous and pushy; from the 17th century

Whirlygig – testicles

Whisker – big lie

Whisker splitter – man of intrigue

White feather – sign of cowardice (it was common practice in the 19th century for men who were regarded as cowards to be given a white feather – the practice was described in moving detail in the novel 'The Four Feathers' by A.E.W.Mason which was first published in 1902 and which has been filmed several times)

White serjeant – man fetched from the pub by his wife was said to have been arrested by the whit serjeant

White soup – stolen silver which has been melted down

White swelling – a pregnant woman is said to have a 'white swelling'

Whitewashed – someone who becomes insolvent to cheat his creditors

Whither-go-ye – wife; this comes from the fact that some wives asked their husbands where they were going when they left the house

Whoa, Emma! – suggestion offered to women behaving strangely in public (often because they were drunk)

Whoever sups with the devil must have a long a spoon – take care when dealing with crooks (or dishonest countries)

Whole hog – bare faced lie, exaggeration (a diner who boasted of eating a great deal of pork was told to go the 'whole hog' and eat the entire pig)

Whore monger – man who keeps more than one mistress

Whore pipe – penis

Whore's kitling –bastard

Widdershins – anticlockwise

Wife in water colours – mistress or concubine

Wild goose chase – tedious and difficult pursuit (geese are notoriously difficult to round up or catch)

Willie-Willie-Wicked-Wicked – this rather strange phrase originated as a reprimand offered to any middle aged woman talking to a youth; the phrase originated with a county court case, related by the wonderful J.Redding Ware in which a middle aged landlady sued a young lodger for a week's rent; his rather bizarre defence was that he left the woman's house because she had a habit of entering his room and sitting on his bed (no explanation was given for his distress, and there was no suggestion of hanky panky)

Windmills in the head – foolish projects

Window – rimless, stringless monocle which young men carried in their right eye, more as a fashion accessory than as an aid to vision

Winter's Day – short and dirty

Wiper – handkerchief

Wiper drawer – pickpocket who specialises in stealing handkerchiefs, particularly silk ones

Without authorial expenses – pirated literary work sold in America

Witling – someone who considers themselves witty and the soul of the party but who is considered by everyone else to a humourless smart aleck

Wobble – boil

Woffle – mask or evade; in musical terms it implied manipulating a difficult passage in a piece of music

Woman of the town – prostitute

Wood pecker – someone who bets on a sport but doesn't play it

Wooden spoon – idiot (the worst students at Cambridge University were given a wooden spoon for their efforts)

Word grubbers – critics, particularly abusive ones (such as trolls perhaps)

Worm eater – man who drills small holes in furniture to give the impression that the item has had woodworm and must be very old

Wreckers – a small group of trouble makers who as part of a first night theatrical audience, deliberately set about making noise and destroying the performance (these were not paid to cause a disturbance but were simply mischief makers); things got so bad that Irving changed his first nights to weekdays; eventually the wreckers were stopped at a performance by Miss Lotta at the Opera Comique in 1883 when friends of the management (including the son of a 'military duke') dealt with the wreckers without recourse to the constabulary or the courts

Wrecking – merciless destruction (taken from the old Cornish custom of using lights to attract ships onto the rocks – and then killing any of the crew who survived, and stealing the cargo); towards the end of the 19th century groups of solicitors made big money by wrecking companies and grabbing whatever they could from the wreckage

Writ pushers – clerks working for lawyers

Wrong side of the hedge – in trouble (originally described passengers who were thrown from the top of a coach, ending up on the wrong side of the hedge)

Wrux – rotter, humbug

Wry neck day – hanging day

X

Xanthippe – woman who gives her husband a bad time; Xanthippe was the wife of Socrates in 5th century BC

Xanthodontous – yellowed teeth; usually from smoking

Xenomania – enthusiasm for things foreign, as opposed to xenophobia

Y

Yaffling – eating
Yard of satin – glass of gin
Yclept – known by the name of, called
Ye Gods and little fishes – expression of contempt
Yellow – to look yellow is to be jealous
Yellow journalism – jingoistic; violent views
Yemeless – careless, negligent (Old English)
Yisse – covet (Middle English word – used between 1150 and 1500)
Yoked – married
You must know Mrs Kelley – something said to long-winded talkers who go on and on; it's meaningless but intended to shut up the speaker
Young person – girl from the age of 15 to marriage
Young thing – youth between the ages of 17 and 21
Younker – youngster; from 16th century
Your head's on fire – comment called out to individuals with red hair; usually by boys or simple minded folk thinking themselves to be witty
You're off the grass – you have no chance (not in the team or, if batting, given out)

Z

Zaftig – having a pleasantly plump figure; shaped like an egg timer
Zeb – best (a piece of Victorian back-slang)
Zeb taoc – best coat (the Victorians rather liked turning words inside out or back to front and this is a good example)

Zedding about – zigzagging

Zedland – those parts of the West Country where the letter z is substituted for the letter s (Devon, Dorset and Somerset)

Zenonian – obstinate

Zest – eagerness

Zounds – a centuries old oath meaning God's wounds

Zucke – withered stump of a tree

Zymurgy – the art of fermentation as in making wine, beer, etc.

Zythespsary – brewery

Zzxjoanw – this word is sometimes listed as meaning a Maori drum but I have more than half a suspicion that it is was created, many years ago, as a hoax to titillate etymologists and delight and frustrate Scrabble players ('Well, it's not in the dictionary so it doesn't count').

The Author

Dr Coleman, a former GP principal, is a Sunday Times bestselling author. His books have sold over three million copies in the UK, been translated into 26 languages and sold all around the world. He has published over 5,000 articles and papers in newspapers, magazines and journals. He was the founding editor of the British Clinical Journal and founded and published the European Medical Journal. Numerous TV and radio series have been based on his books. His novel 'Mrs Caldicot's Cabbage War' (about the oppression and mistreatment of the elderly) was turned into a highly successful, award winning film. In the UK, he has given evidence to the House of Commons and the House of Lords and his campaigning have over many decades changed Government policy. He has lectured doctors and nurses in numerous countries. There is an up-to-date list of his books on www.vernoncoleman.com where there are also many articles to read and videos to view. The site has no pay wall and all articles and videos are free and do not carry advertisements.